Beneath the Carolina Sun

the

Carolina Sun

Sandy Island

ASHLEY
FARLEY

also by ashley farley

Sandy Island

Southern Discomfort

Beneath the Carolina Sun

Marsh Point

Long Journey Home

Echoes of the Past

Songbird's Second Chance

Heart of Lowcountry

After the Storm

Scent of Magnolia

Virginia Vineyards

Love Child

Blind Love

Forbidden Love

Love and War

Palmetto Island

Muddy Bottom

Change of Tides

Lowcountry on My Mind

Sail Away

Hope Springs Series

Dream Big, Stella!

Show Me the Way

Mistletoe and Wedding Bells

Matters of the Heart

Road to New Beginnings

Stand Alone

On My Terms

Tangled in Ivy

Lies that Bind

Life on Loan

Only One Life

Home for Wounded Hearts

Nell and Lady

Sweet Tea Tuesdays

Saving Ben

Sweeney Sisters Series

Saturdays at Sweeney's

Tangle of Strings

Boots and Bedlam

Lowcountry Stranger

Her Sister's Shoes

Magnolia Series

Beyond the Garden

Magnolia Nights

Scottie's Adventures

Breaking the Story

Merry Mary

one

· · ·

P eace settled over Magnolia Shores as Kate waved goodbye to the last guest at the end of the Fourth of July weekend. The bed and breakfast had been a hubbub of activity for the past five days, bustling with young families participating in various events. Kate smiled to herself as her thoughts drifted to her father. Edward St. Clair had dreamed of sharing their family's hundred-acre compound with the world. Turning their oceanfront home into a bed and breakfast was the first step in realizing that vision. He would have relished seeing his beloved home enjoyed to the fullest.

Needing time alone, Kate grabbed her sketchbook from the cottage she shared with her mother and headed to the beach. Seated under an umbrella with her toes digging in the sand, she sketched out the brass pendant she'd been contemplating these past few days. As the leading salesperson for Texas's most prominent lighting distributor, Kate had a deep understanding of what wealthy customers sought in high-end fixtures. Her goal was to one day bring her designs to life.

Kate was so immersed in her task that she failed to notice her brother's approach. Pritchard opened his beach chair and plopped down beside her. "I see you haven't abandoned your favorite hobby."

"Nope. Drawing relaxes me and satisfies my creative side." She closed the cover of her sketchbook. Even as a child, she'd been too hypercritical of her work to share it with anyone. "What're you up to today?"

"I stopped by to see Mother, but she's asleep." Pritchard tugged his shirt over his head. His shoulders were still broad, and his arms muscular. But his chest hair had begun to gray, and his waist had thickened. The years had flown by, and they'd landed in middle age. "I'm glad I ran into you. Saves me a phone call. I'm meeting with Ashton tomorrow morning at nine. She will present her plans for The Sanctuary, and I'd like you to join us."

Ashton was his sister-in-law and the architect of their proposed expansion project.

"There you go, tempting me again. You don't need my input, Pritchard. This is your project."

"You're part owner of Magnolia Shores whether or not you're involved with managing the resort. I need your blessing before moving forward with construction." He lifted his sunglasses to reveal twinkling blue eyes. "Besides, I don't think it would take much to tempt you."

"What's that supposed to mean?"

"For weeks, you've been saying you need to return to your life in Texas, yet you've made no move to leave the Lowcountry."

Kate adjusted her straw hat, shading her auburn hair from the sun. "I wanted to enjoy the holiday.I haven't spent July Fourth here in years. Besides, I've been wrapping up loose ends for Mom."

He pushed his sunglasses back into position and settled in his chair. "Thank you for lining up her caregivers, by the way. Mom has enjoyed having you around. She'll miss you when you're gone."

A soft smile curved Kate's lip. "I'll miss her too. And you're welcome. I'm glad to help, especially since you're responsible for her most of the time."

"She appears to be on the path to a full recovery," Pritchard said, tilting his face to the sun.

"I think so too. Her physical therapy is going well. She'll soon be able to trade her walker for a cane, and her speech is slowly but surely getting better." Kate took a long drink from her water bottle. "But you're right. Now that the Fourth is over, nothing is keeping me here. I need to get back to my job and the preparations for Grace's wedding."

"You sound thrilled," Pritchard said in a sarcastic tone.

She *wasn't* thrilled about going home, but she had responsibilities in Texas she could no longer ignore, like dealing with the young woman covering for her at work whom Kate suspected was trying to steal her job.

"We almost lost Mama. I'm hesitant to leave for fear she might have another stroke."

"That possibility will always exist, Kate. But you can't put your life on hold for something that may never happen. Look on the bright side. I'm sure Rand will be happy to see you."

Kate wasn't so sure about that. Her marriage had been on the rocks for years, and they'd both needed this time apart. She hadn't heard from Rand in the weeks since her mother regained consciousness. Was there more to her husband's silence than his hectic schedule as a cardiac surgeon? She'd been hiding out in the Lowcountry, and the time to face her marital problems had come. She would book a flight for the end of the week.

Kate nudged her brother's leg with her foot. "I feel like a swim. I'll race you to the pool."

He sat up straight. "You're on."

Scrambling out of their chairs, they took off, running up the path through the dunes to the pool. After rinsing the sand off their feet, they dove into the pool and swam underwater to the other end. Pritchard scrambled on top of a raft, declaring himself King of the Mountain, and they fought for the coveted position until they were both exhausted. They climbed out of the pool and stretched out flat on the deck, staring up at the sky.

Kate rolled her head to the side, looking over at her brother. "That was awesome. I can't remember when I've had so much fun."

Pritchard laughed. "Right? This grown-up stuff is for the birds. I'd give anything to relive my childhood."

Kate thought about it for a minute. While there was much she preferred to forget, she would gladly revisit many aspects of her childhood. "What do you miss the most?"

"Mm," he hesitated, thinking. "Picnics and bonfires on the beach, water skiing and sailing, but mostly, I miss Mom, the way she used to be."

Kate sat up, tucking her knees to her chest. "She was a much happier person back then," she said. *Until the event that shaped all their lives happened.*

With a pang of guilt, she stood up and grabbed towels from the wooden hut where they stored beach chairs and pool gear. After drying off, each wrapped a towel around themself and walked together through the manicured garden that separated the main house from the outbuildings. The pool and garden houses, miniature versions of the main house, each offered five guest rooms and communal living quarters—a sitting room, kitchenette, and small dining area.

Kate paused to smell a pink rose. "All good things must come to an end, but I plan to enjoy my last days in the Lowcountry to the fullest. I want to spend every moment I can with Mom and Shelby." Kate's youngest daughter, a Texas A&M hospitality graduate, moved to South Carolina to assist her mom in opening the bed and breakfast. Shelby, who had thrived here during childhood summers, now embraced the Lowcountry as her permanent home, much to Kate's joy.

"I've enjoyed our time together, Kate. I didn't realize how much I've missed our friendship."

Kate pinched off a rose petal and handed it to him. "We were a formidable team, the dynamic brother-sister duo, during our youth. We've never talked about what happened. Are you still upset with me for taking Mom's side when you wanted to marry Savannah?"

"Not at all. You got caught in the middle. You were concerned about me, and I appreciate that. Savannah and I were too young to be parents. But she was pregnant with my child, I was crazy in love with her, and I wanted to do the honorable thing by marrying her. We could've made it work, but Mom made sure I never got the chance." His gaze shifted to the cottage where their mom was napping. "I forgave her a long time ago for breaking Savannah and me up, but . . ." His voice trailed off.

"But what? What's causing the tension between you and Mom now?"

"Mom was awful to Savannah when she first came back to town. And Harper, too, her own granddaughter."

"I think Mom is trying," Kate said. "She's been more pleasant since her stroke."

"And I should be grateful for that. It just shouldn't have to be that hard. Savannah and I reunited after thirty years apart, and we found our long-lost child. Why wouldn't she be happy for us?"

"Mom is a complicated person, Pritch. I stopped trying to figure her out long ago." They circled the small fountain and continued across the cobblestone courtyard toward the cottage. "These past few weeks, I've seen glimpses of the old Mom from our childhood. Maybe she learned something from her near-death experience."

"Maybe. We'll see if it lasts."

Kate reached for the doorknob. "Have you seen what Harper has done to the cottage?"

"No, but she's told me about it."

When they entered the cottage, their mother's caregiver pressed her finger to her lips, letting them know their Mom was still asleep.

Pritchard's daughter, who had recently purchased a local interior design firm, had worked wonders with the outdated interior. She'd replaced the yellowed linoleum flooring with laminate hardwoods and swapped the outdated plaid couch for a khaki linen-covered sectional. The kitchen cabinets had been refreshed with a coat of high-gloss white paint and new stainless-steel appliances were installed. Sisal rugs now covered the bedroom and sitting room floors, the windows sported woven shades, and a pair of blue and white lamps adorned the tables at both ends of the sofa.

"This looks amazing," Pritchard said in a soft voice. "It's cheerful but cozy. What does Mom think?"

Kate shrugged. "I think she likes it, but it's hard to say with Mom."

Pritchard's phone buzzed in his hand. "I should go. Savannah's waiting for me to start the grill."

Kate walked him to the door. "Thanks for carving out some time for me today. I'll be at the meeting tomorrow and look forward to seeing Ashton's designs."

"I agree. Today was nice," he said, kissing her forehead.

Despondency overcame Kate as she watched him drive away in his Audi. These past weeks had provided a renewed sense of self. How could she possibly leave her family or the Lowcountry?

Shelby followed the boat's progress as it sped across Catawba Sound toward her. Although the guy driving looked like Matt, the skiff was much smaller than Matt's center console. A cooler doubled as a seat in front of the steering console, and a platform stretched across the stern in front of the outboard engine.

Matt and Shelby often spent the evening hours together on his boat, with him fishing and her reading a paperback romance on the bow. As he drew near, she noticed two fishing rods in the rod holders. Surely, he wasn't expecting her to use one.

"Afternoon, kiddo!" he called out as he nosed his boat to the dock.

"Afternoon, old man," she shot back as she stepped onto the boat's bow. Their seven-year age difference—her twenty-four years to his thirty-one—had become a sore subject between them. They'd had a brief fling when they first met at the beginning of the summer, but despite their undeniable chemistry, they'd agreed to be just friends. Matt thought she was too young, and Shelby was reluctant to commit after her breakup with a long-time boyfriend. But try as she might, she couldn't deny her attraction to him.

"Whose boat is this?" Shelby asked.

"My next-door neighbor's. We swapped boats for the evening. The flood tide is ideal for spot fishing in the flats, but my boat is too large to navigate the marsh. He agreed readily since his in-laws are in town, and he wanted to use my boat for a sightseeing tour of Catawba Sound."

Shelby gestured at the rods. "Cool! What's with the second fishing pole?"

"It's not a pole, Shelby. It's a fly-fishing rod. I brought an extra one for you."

Shelby shook her head. "No way! I told you, I'm not into fishing."

"Sight fishing is different. The flood tide almost guarantees success."

Shelby sat down on the cooler as Matt navigated away from the dock. He picked up speed as they headed south toward the marshland and rode silently through the winding creeks. The world stilled when Matt killed the engine and sweat dotted her forehead.

"Geez," Shelby said, fanning her face. "It's hot back in here. I like the ocean better."

"The ocean is too rough today." He handed her a fly-fishing rod. "It's all rigged up and ready to go."

Shelby removed her rom-com from her tote bag. "No thanks.

I'd rather read my book." Her grandfather had taught her to fish as a child, and while she enjoyed being on the water with him, reeling in fish never did much for her.

"Give me that," Matt said, snatching the book from her and placing it behind the console's windshield. "This is a different kind of fishing. Here, I'll show you. We're fishing for red drum. You will see their tails skim the water's surface as they feed."

Shelby looked down at the water. "I can't see anything."

"You won't with those sunglasses. Here." He slid her sunglasses off her face, replacing them with frames equipped with polarized lenses. "There. Now look into the water."

She peered over the side. "Wow. You're right. I can see the bottom."

"Exactly. Now, when you spot a fish, the goal is to cast your fly so that it lands a few feet in front of him."

"How do you know it's a him?"

"Be serious, Shelby," he said, handing her the rod.

She handed it back to him. "I'll sit this one out. My grandfather tried to teach me to fly fish. It didn't go well."

"I'm not letting you give up until you try," he said, positioning the rod in her hands and wrapping his arms around her from behind.

Shelby silently cursed their platonic relationship. His ruggedness drove her wild. His rock-solid body and strong muscles made her feel safe, while the lingering scent of fresh air and salt water on him sent waves of pleasure through her. She didn't even mind the permanent dirt under his fingernails. Luke, her previous boyfriend since middle school, was a bougie boy in skinny jeans, driving loafers, and gel-styled hair. When Shelby was ready to try again, she would look for an outdoorsy Lowcountry boy—someone younger and less domineering than Matt.

Shelby spotted a fish and let out a squeal. "There's one!"

"Shh!" Matt whispered in her ear. "I see him. Be quiet before you scare him off. Now, let's present the fly." Matt guided her hand as they cast the fly a few feet in front of the fish. He dropped his arm from around her and stepped back. "Now strip your line with gentle tugs so the fish thinks the fly is skimming the water."

Shelby followed his instructions and watched in amazement as the fish swam toward the fly. It pulled on the line as it bit down on the fly.

"Now reel him in," Matt encouraged.

The fish fought against her, but she persisted until Matt had netted him.

"I did it!" she hollered.

"Yes, you did," Matt replied, offering her a high five. He carefully removed the hook and held the fish out to her. "Now, hold him while I take your picture."

Shelby eyed the fish skeptically. "No way! I'm not touching that slimy thing."

"Come on, Shelby. I didn't take you for a sissy."

"Fine. Let me fix my hair." She tugged her unkempt strawberry-blonde hair free of the elastic band.

Matt let out a low whistle. "Wow. I love it when you wear your hair down." He was good for her ego, often complimenting her on her hair and the freckles dotting her face.

"If only I weren't so young, right?" She held out her hands. "Now, give me the poor fish before he dies."

He gently placed the fish in her hands, quickly snapped a picture, and then carefully returned the fish to the water. "Are you ready to try again?"

"Sure! That was fun."

Matt tied a new fly on the end of the line and handed her the rod. "You're on your own." He stood in position on the platform and paddled the boat close to the marsh to search for fish.

They took turns reeling them in for two more hours until the tide changed, and the fish stopped biting.

"I've worked up an appetite," he said as he secured his rods in the rod holders. "Wanna grab some dinner at Comet Dogs?"

Shelby groaned at his suggestion. She enjoyed teasing him

about his favorite eatery, but she secretly loved the gourmet hot dogs. Her favorite was the Chili Cheddar Dog Deluxe—an all-beef dog smothered in chili and cheddar cheese with grilled onions and dill relish.

After packing up their fishing gear, Matt navigated the boat out of the marsh and across Catawba Sound to the small town's waterfront shopping and restaurant district. They placed their order and sat down at a picnic table in the shade of a live oak tree. Matt laughed at her when she cut her hot dog with a knife and fork.

"Why is that so funny?" she asked. "It's too messy to eat like a normal hot dog."

"You mean like this?" he said, taking a bite of his hot dog.

"Exactly. If you could see yourself in the mirror," Shelby said, jabbing her plastic fork at him. "You have chili all over your face."

He wiped his face with his napkin and took another bite. "How was your weekend at the B&B? Did your guests behave?"

"Yep. Although we had a lot of families with little kids, surprisingly, none of them got out of line. Most of the guests checked out today. We'll have a break for a few days, but more guests will arrive on Wednesday for next weekend." She sipped her lemonade. "How was *your* weekend?"

"Excellent. I fished all weekend."

Shelby rolled her eyes. "Of course you did. Do you have a busy week ahead?"

"I think so. Will is starting renovations on a historic home. The demo begins tomorrow. He's putting me in charge of our summer hires."

Shelby's face lit up. She knew how eager he was for a management position at Darby Custom Homes. "Good for you!"

They talked about their fishing expedition while they finished eating. Matt called her a natural and promised to teach her how to catch different species of fish. When he dropped her off at the dock later, he didn't mention seeing her again, which was unusual. They typically made plans for the next outing. She shrugged it off, assuming he was preoccupied with the demolition job ahead. But the prospect of not seeing him again anytime soon disappointed her more than it should. His companionship alleviated the ache of the emptiness she felt inside.

two

. . .

G race watched her fiancé watching the one-year-old toddle among the adults gathered to celebrate his first birthday. Wyatt was enamored of his godchild. He never stopped talking about him—Colton did this, and Colton did that. And he spoiled the kid rotten, buying him gifts for no particular reason. Grace wanted children but planned to wait until her early thirties to get pregnant. She'd rather be spending her Sunday afternoon anywhere else. Even pulling weeds held more appeal than a kid's birthday party. Grace wasn't close friends with Colton's mother. Tasha's squeaky voice and fake niceness grated on Grace's nerves, but because Tasha was married to Wyatt's best friend, Grace had no choice but to make nice back.

Looking away from the child, Grace took in her surroundings. She much preferred the charming, restored craftsman-style house she shared with Wyatt over Tasha's new construction McMansion. Although she admitted Tasha had done an excellent job designing their new patio, which featured a built-in grill, seating area, and fireplace. Grace and Wyatt were currently saving for a kitchen and family room addition. Depending on the size of their next bonuses, they might be able to afford a similar outdoor living space.

After the cake ritual ended, Grace used the excuse of needing to do laundry to insist they leave.

"That kid is so darn cute," Wyatt said as they pulled out of the driveway. "I can't wait to get this wedding over with so we can start our own family."

"April will be here before you know it," Grace muttered, biting back her irritation. She was fed up with him constantly dissing their wedding.

He glanced over at her. "April is nine months away. We could have a baby by then."

"You know how I feel, Wyatt. I want to meet certain career milestones before I have children." She stared out the window at the passing trees. "Why are you always so negative about our wedding?"

He tightened his grip on the steering wheel. "Because I never agreed to such a large production."

A production? Grace thought, her irritation morphing into anger. "Geez, Wyatt. You make it sound like a three-ring circus. I'm working hard to make our wedding an elegant affair."

His shoulders slumped. "I just wish you had consulted me. I hate how consumed you've become by all the planning."

"I agree it's a lot. Mom should be helping me. She says she's coming home from South Carolina soon."

"For your sake, I hope she means it," he grumbled as he pulled into their driveway.

Grace gathered her belongings. "I didn't eat much at the party. I'm going to make a salad. Do you want one? We could open a bottle of wine and sit on the porch."

He opened his car door and threw one long leg out. "Thanks, but I had plenty to eat. And I need to finish up some work before tomorrow. I thought you had to do laundry anyway."

"I can multitask, Wyatt."

They entered the house, and he retreated to the home office they shared. Shelby poured a glass of white wine from the open bottle in the refrigerator and grabbed a bag of Skinny Pop from the pantry. Taking her latest issues of bridal magazines to the table on the covered porch, she opened the Google Document containing her wedding task list. Her top priority was making a deposit on the funk band they'd booked for the reception. She also needed to choose a color for the bridesmaids' dresses, book cake tastings with the area's top bakeries, send out the save-the-date cards, and order the invitations. When she asked Wyatt to help her with the gift registry, he'd told her to choose whatever she wanted. She had so much to do with no one to help her. Picking up her phone, she texted her mother.

> I really need help with this wedding. When are you coming home?

Her mother texted back.

> Soon.

On Monday morning, Grace woke in a cold sweat from a nightmare about her wedding. In the dream, she'd neglected to order the bridesmaids' dresses, and her friends had all shown up for the ceremony in their pajamas.

Freeing her body from the tangled sheets, she showered and dressed for work. She then put on coffee to brew while rummaging through the kitchen drawers for her misplaced fabric swatches.

"What're you looking for?" Wyatt asked from the doorway.

"Fabric swatches for my bridesmaids' dresses. Have you seen them? I can't find them anywhere."

"Um, no. Why would I have seen them?"

"Because you live here too," Grace snapped, opening and closing another row of drawers.

Wyatt grabbed her by the arm, spinning her away from the

drawers. "Look at you, Grace. You're working yourself into a panic over some dumb fabric swatches. This is what I meant when I said you were consumed. You give new meaning to the word *Bridezilla*. I seriously can't take this anymore."

Grace wrenched her arm free. "What's that supposed to mean?"

"I can't be around you right now. I should stay with my parents until after the wedding."

Grace glared at him. "Things wouldn't be so bad if I had some help."

"Since your mom doesn't appear to be coming home anytime soon, why don't you take a couple of days off and fly to South Carolina? The fresh, salty air would clear your head. You can call it a wedding planning retreat."

Grace considered his idea. With Kate's undivided attention, the two of them could accomplish a lot in a short amount of time. "Maybe I will," she huffed.

"I'm only trying to help, Grace. You've been so touchy lately, I can't even offer suggestions," he said, turning away from her and heading toward the front door.

Grabbing her purse, she left the house behind him. She clicked on her mother's number as she walked to her car. When Kate didn't pick up, she left a message. "Hey, Mom, it's me. Do you know where the swatches are for the bridesmaids' dresses? I'm freaking out here. We need to order the dresses ASAP. Please call me."

On her way to work, Grace detoured by her parents' house to look for the swatches. She was surprised to see her father's Mercedes convertible parked in the driveway. He usually kept it in the garage. When she let herself in the front door, she heard the shower running overhead in her parents' bedroom. She located the swatches in the top right drawer of her mother's desk and spread them out at the kitchen table to study them. Pink was too prissy. She was naturally inclined toward shades of blues, but apple green would be lovely for an April wedding.

Grace jerked her head up at the sound of footsteps descending the stairs. If her father was in the shower, who could it be? She gasped as her mom's best friend appeared in the doorway, wearing a bathrobe. Wasn't that Grace's mother's bathrobe? "Claudia? What're you doing here?"

Claudia's face beamed red as she glanced nervously toward the stairs. "Your mom borrowed a dress from me. I wanted to wear it to a party tonight. I was just looking for it in Kate's closet."

Grace eyed the bathrobe. "I see you found her bathrobe instead?"

"I . . . um . . ."

Grace got to her feet and crossed the room in three strides. "How long have you been having an affair with my father?" She jabbed a finger at Claudia's face. "And don't even think about lying to me because I caught you red-handed."

Claudia straightened, tying the robe tighter around her. "It only happened this once. We just hooked up, as you young people like to say. Your mom's out of town, and Bobby had to fly to California on business. I ran into your father at the club last night. We had a few drinks. One thing led to another, and here we are."

Grace set her slate-blue eyes on Claudia. "I don't believe you. I'm your goddaughter. You'd better tell me the truth. Are you having an affair with my father?"

Claudia waved dismissively. "So maybe we hooked up a few times. But who's counting? We've both been lonely with our spouses out of town. You're too young to understand, but when adults reach middle age, we sometimes need a little something to spice up our lives."

Grace gawked at her. "*A little something?* Why not take up a new exercise routine or find a hobby? You don't sleep with your best friend's husband just because you're bored. You should be ashamed of yourself, Claudia."

"Where's the harm if no one gets hurt? Your father and I love our spouses. Neither of us wants a divorce. Can I count on you to keep this between us?"

"Have you lost your mind? I have no intention of keeping your dirty little secret. I'm telling Mom as soon as I get her on the phone," Grace said, snatching up the swatches and storming out of the house.

She dialed her mom's number as she peeled off down the road. Kate didn't answer, and she tried calling five more times. Realizing she was driving on the wrong side of the street, she swerved back into her lane and tossed her phone into the cupholder.

A range of emotions overwhelmed her—anger, disbelief, and disappointment. Her father, a handsome and successful cardiac surgeon, undoubtedly had attractive nurses throwing themselves at him all the time. But he was a principled man, committed to his wife and family. She never imagined him the type to have an affair—and certainly not with his wife's best friend.

three

· · ·

Kate prepared a continental breakfast for the B&B guests while her mom read the newspaper at the worn pine table, where they had eaten all their family meals during her youth. "What's on your agenda today, Izzy?" Kate asked.

"Physical torture," Izzy grunted without looking up from the paper. She complained about her hours-long physical therapy sessions, but the so-called torture was working wonders to restore her strength.

Her mother had insisted that her grandchildren call her Izzy, short for Isabelle, instead of Grandmother or Nana. The name had stuck, and now family and close friends all referred to her as Izzy.

Blossom bustled through the back door with her miniature basset hound at her feet. She wore white linen blousy pants and a pale-pink tunic with a bright-pink hibiscus flower tucked in her messy knot of silver coils. "Morning, ladies," she said as she set out bowls of water and dog food for Jolene.

"Morning," Izzy and Kate said in unison.

Kate made several trips to the dining room, delivering trays of pastries, mini quiches, and a bowl of fresh fruit to the buffet. Once everything was in order, she returned to the kitchen, poured herself a mug of coffee, and joined Blossom and Izzy at the table. Kate studied Blossom as she sipped her coffee. She was struck, as always, by the woman's ethereal beauty, clear emerald eyes and flawless caramel skin.

"So, Blossom, how long are you staying at Magnolia Shores?" Kate asked.

Blossom raised a manicured eyebrow. "I booked my room for the entire summer. I thought you knew that."

Kate smiled. "I did. And I certainly love having you around. I just figured you'd be taking off now that your mission is complete."

"My mission isn't quite complete. I still have one final matter to attend to." Blossom nudged Izzy's arm. "I believe you have something to discuss with your daughter."

Izzy set down the newspaper. One side of her mouth lifted as her words tumbled out. "Can you . . . plan a . . . family dinner . . . for tomorrow . . . night?"

Blossom patted Izzy's hand as though congratulating her on a job well done. "This dinner is important to your mama. We thought it best to wrap up this loose end before your new guests check in on Wednesday. I'll take care of the meal if you make sure everyone can come."

Kate glanced at the wall clock. "I'm meeting with Pritchard and Shelby in a few minutes. I'll ask them if they're free."

Izzy furrowed her gray brow. "Meeting?"

"Pritchard's sister-in-law, Ashton, is presenting her plans for The Sanctuary. You're welcome to join us," Kate said, even though she wasn't sure her brother was ready for their mother to see the plans.

Izzy let out a humph. "Monstrosity! Will obstruct . . . my view . . . of oc-ean," she said, struggling to get out the last word.

"I highly doubt that. You live on the southern tip of Sandy Island with a 280-degree view of the ocean and sound." Kate's expression became serious. "I admit I'm worried this new building will negatively impact our landscape. I'd hate to ruin the unspoiled natural beauty of Magnolia Shores."

Blossom sat back in her chair and massaged her chin in thought. "A lot depends on the style of your building. Incorporating the environment into the design could yield a pleasing result."

Kate's yellow-green eyes widened. "I hadn't thought of that, but you're right, Blossom. I've been envisioning a simple rectangular building, a monolithic block. A structure with porches, awnings, and a multitiered roof could add charm to the property."

Her father had left explicit instructions in his will for their family's historic home to be turned into a bed and breakfast. They recently discovered his journal detailing plans for expanding the bed and breakfast into a boutique resort.

The faint sound of voices wafted down the hall from the foyer. Kate sat up in her chair. "I'm suddenly eager to see Ashton's plans. Can you hold down the fort while I meet with them?"

Izzy nodded, and Blossom shooed her away. "Go on, love bug. I'll stay with your mama in case your guests need anything."

"Thank you, Blossom." Topping off her coffee, Kate headed down the hall to the foyer, admiring the worn oak floors and priceless antiques. While Kate would have no official role in running the resort, she felt inclined to participate in the planning to ensure the new building met their family's high standards.

Kate greeted Ashton with a hug. "This is exciting. I can't wait to see what you've come up with."

Ashton shivered. "I don't know why I'm a nervous wreck. I've presented countless designs to clients. I'm worried about doing justice to the property's significant historical value."

Pritchard smiled. "I have faith in you, Ashton. You've become the most sought-after architect in the Lowcountry. Shall we," he said, motioning them to walk ahead of him through the living room to his father's study.

Shelby was already there, seated behind the massive

mahogany desk she had cleared to make room for the blueprints. Ashton unrolled the designs on the desk to reveal a computer-generated elevation featuring a sprawling three-story building with porches, awnings, and a grand entrance reminiscent of an elegant old Floridian hotel.

Shelby gasped. "It's a longer, taller version of the main house."

Ashton beamed. "That was my goal. Do you like it?"

"It's gorgeous. I love it." Kate craned her neck to see Pritchard standing behind her. "What do you think?"

"I'm speechless." Pritchard paused while he studied the drawing. "I wasn't sure what to expect. But this is stunning. I wish Dad were here to see this."

They gathered around the desk while Ashton showed them the blueprints for the three floors. The ground level featured a large reception area, lobby, dining room, cocktail lounge, upscale gift shop, and spa with a fitness center. The second and third floors housed thirty guest suites with marble bathrooms, spa tubs, and balconies.

Pritchard placed a hand on the architect's shoulder. "You've outdone yourself, Ashton. I'm truly blown away, but it's way more elaborate than I expected, and I'm not sure we can afford to build it."

Ashton tapped her fingernail on the blueprints. "Either build this or don't build at all. If you settle for anything less, you will be doing a disservice to this magnificent property."

He gave her a curt nod. "You have a point."

Ashton sat down on the edge of the desk. "I suggest you get other bids, but Will wants this project. We've discussed the plans at length, and he'll match any price you get."

"Will's reputation speaks for itself. And I'd rather keep it in the family," Pritchard said.

Ashton nodded. "He and I work well together. We've discussed scheduling. If we break ground right after Labor Day, assuming you close the bed and breakfast for the winter, we'll be finished in time to reopen before next summer."

"Why do we have to close the bed and breakfast?" Shelby asked.

"Having guests around will significantly slow us down."

"How much time are you talking?" Kate asked.

Ashton shrugged. "Hard to say. Six months. A year."

Pritchard's gaze shifted to Shelby. "What do our reservations look like for the fall?"

"I've had a lot of inquiries but only a few bookings," Shelby said.

Pritchard rubbed the back of his neck. "This is a lot to absorb. I realize we must act quickly, but give us a couple of days to mull it over."

Ashton gestured at the blueprints. "Of course. These are your copies. Call me anytime with questions. We can arrange another meeting if further discussion is helpful."

Kate tugged her vibrating phone out of her pocket, surprised to see she had five missed calls from Grace. "Excuse me a minute," she said to the others and stepped outside the French doors to the terrace.

Dread overcame her as she answered Grace's call. Although her oldest daughter texted all the time, she only called when something was wrong. "What is it, Grace? What's happened?"

"Mom . . . um . . ."

"Grace? Hello? Are you still there?" Kate could tell from the background noise that they were still connected, and Grace was in her car listening to the call on Bluetooth. "You're scaring me, Grace. What's going on?"

"Sorry, Mom. I was distracted by traffic. I was looking for the fabric samples for the bridesmaids' dresses. But I found them, so never mind."

"I'm glad you found them. But is that really why you called me six times?"

"Duh. I need to pick a color so my bridesmaids can order their dresses."

Grace sounded on the verge of tears, which heightened Kate's concern to alarm. Her eldest never cried. "What's wrong, sweetheart? You don't sound right."

"I'm super stressed about this wedding. Have you booked your flight home?"

"Not yet. But the wedding isn't until April. We have months left to get things done." After seeing Ashton's plans for The Sanctuary, she was more dubious than ever about leaving Magnolia Shores. She felt more excited about the expansion than anything in years.

"Get home as soon as you can. I need you," Grace said and hung up on her.

Guilt tightened Kate's chest as she pocketed the phone. Her daughter needed her. She should be on a plane headed back to Texas. Someone always needed her. Would she ever be able to focus on her own life?

Kate paused to compose herself before returning to her father's study. Ashton had gone, and Pritchard and Shelby were discussing closing down the bed and breakfast for the winter.

"I'll go crazy here with nothing to do," Shelby complained.

"You'll be on paid leave for the fall. Next spring, you'll be busy hiring and training the new staff." Pritchard squeezed her shoulder. "Let's not get ahead of ourselves. First, we must decide if we're moving forward with this expansion."

"I guess you're right." Shelby glanced over at Kate and frowned. "Mom, are you okay? You don't look so good."

Kate smiled softly at her daughter. "I'm fine, sweetheart."

"Who were you talking to on the phone?"

"Grace. She needs my help with the wedding."

Shelby rolled her eyes. "Can't she do anything for herself?"

Kate ignored her comment. "Ashton's designs are outstanding. Where do we go from here?" she asked her brother.

Pritchard rolled up the blueprints and slid them back into the cardboard tube. "I've already scheduled a meeting with Will for tomorrow morning. Before we move forward, I need him to give me an idea of how much a building of this complexity will cost."

"Good. Report back to us when you come for dinner tomorrow night. Mom has requested our presence. And that includes Savannah and Harper."

Pritchard groaned. "I'll ask them. But I'm not making any promises."

"Try hard, Pritch. I'm not sure what Mom has in mind, but I get the impression this dinner is important to her."

Family meant everything to Pritchard, and the friction between their mother, his wife, and his daughter was taking a toll on him. Izzy had been on the verge of apologizing, the first step to making amends, when she suffered a stroke.

After seeing Pritchard out, Kate returned to her mother in the kitchen. Izzy pointed at a vacant chair. "Tell me."

Kate dropped down to the chair. "This is probably not what you want to hear, but the design is spectacular. I believe even you would approve."

Izzy reached for Kate's hand, giving it a weak squeeze. "You're glowing, the happiest I've seen you in years. You belong here." She struggled with her words, but her determined expression told Kate she had more to say.

"My life is in Texas, Mama."

"But is that life happy? You seemed so des-pon-dent when you first came." Izzy placed her hand on Kate's cheek. "You've trans-formed into the ex-u-ber-ant girl of your youth." She paused to breathe. Speaking took so much out of her.

"I appreciate what you're trying to say, but save your strength, Mama. I have responsibilities in Texas."

"You've raised your children. Now it's your turn to take care of yourself."

"I'm married, remember? Randall has a thriving medical practice in Austin. He can't just up and move."

Izzy removed her hand from Kate's face. "Then leave him in Texas."

"Mom! You know I can't do that." Although Kate had never mentioned her marital problems, her mother had keen intuition about her only daughter. Kate believed her marriage was salvageable. She and Rand simply needed to spend more time together, to reconnect and rediscover each other. Now that their nest was empty, they needed to figure out how to be a couple again.

four

. . .

Grace had been on the verge of telling her mother about her father's affair—his so-called fleeting indiscretion—when she realized she couldn't deliver such devastating news over the phone. If she took Wyatt's advice and flew to South Carolina, she could kill two birds with one stone. She'd been worried about her grandmother since the stroke and relished the opportunity to visit with Izzy. She would have a long wedding planning session with her mother, and afterward, she would break the news about her father's affair with Claudia.

Grace gripped the steering wheel and floored the gas pedal, speeding through the downtown streets to her office. An exemplary employee dedicated to her career as an artificial intelligence engineer, she worked long hours and never missed a deadline. When she explained about a family emergency, her boss readily agreed to her requested paid time off. Grace booked her flight, gathered her belongings from her office, and rushed home to pack.

She arrived at the airport as her flight was boarding. Although she rarely acted on a whim, she felt good about her decision to make this trip. She was buckled into her first-class seat, sipping a glass of Champagne and scrolling through her emails, when she received a long text from Claudia.

> Think of what a messy divorce would do to your wedding. Your parents are already arguing over the expense of your elaborate reception. If you betray him, your father might decide not to pay for any of it. I know how much you want him to walk you down the aisle. I haven't told Rand about our run-in this morning. For everyone's sake, I suggest we keep this between us. You have my word that I won't sleep with your father again.

Grace thumbed off her response.

> Your word is worthless. I'm on a plane now, headed to South Carolina to see Mom.

Dropping her phone in her lap, she stared out the window as the plane accelerated down the runway. Claudia was right. A divorce would ruin her wedding. Her mother would be a wreck, too preoccupied with living arrangements, separation agreements, and financial settlements to focus on the wedding. This meaningless affair could potentially destroy Grace's wedding, her parents' thirty-year marriage, and her mother's long-term friendship with Claudia. What Kate doesn't know won't hurt her. Right?

Grace was already in the air. There was no turning back now. She might as well enjoy a few days in the Lowcountry with her mother and grandmother. She would have plenty of time with Kate to make decisions regarding the wedding. Besides, Grace was overdue for some rest and relaxation. She would sit on the beach and read a book. Wyatt would miss her, and when she finally returned home, he would welcome her with open arms.

Grace rested her head against the seat and closed her eyes. The case was closed. Her father's affair with Claudia was forgotten. Ha. If only life were that easy.

Shelby sat at the kitchen table, staring at her phone and willing a text from Matt to appear. With only a few guests in-house, she'd been bored out of her mind most of the day. She longed to go for a boat ride in the ocean or to try her hand at fly-fishing again. She would even settle for dinner at Comet Dogs.

Inhaling a deep breath for courage, she typed a message to him.

> Hey. Wanna come over for dinner? I can run to the seafood market for tuna steaks.

She crossed her fingers, waiting for his response. Matt loved seafood, and she couldn't imagine him passing up a tuna steak. But when her phone pinged, her heart sank at his response.

> Sorry, kiddo. I have a date tonight. Another time maybe.

Tears blurred her vision as she thumbed off several messages before deciding on the right tone.

> Good for you! Who's the lucky girl?

> Someone I met on Hinge.

Shelby tossed the phone on the table. He never mentioned having a profile on a dating app. He had put himself on the market. He was looking for romance. Which meant he'd given up on having a relationship with Shelby.

The back door swung open, and Blossom entered the kitchen,

her arms laden with grocery bags. "Why the long face, baby girl?" she asked, setting the bags on the counter.

"I invited Matt to come over for dinner, but he has a date."

Blossom dragged a chair over next to Shelby. "I'm sorry, honey. I can see you're upset, but I thought you two decided to just be friends."

Shelby bit down on her quivering lower lip. "We agreed to be friends while I sorted myself out. He told me he'd wait as long as it took. That was only a few weeks ago. Something happened to change his mind. He thinks I'm too young for him. Or maybe he hates my freckles."

Blossom thumbed a tear off her cheek. "He loves your freckles. We all love your freckles. You have to stop blaming your freckles whenever something doesn't go your way."

"Blaming my freckles is easier than admitting I'm unlovable."

"You're talking nonsense, baby girl," Blossom said, putting her arms around Shelby and pulling her close.

"I'm so tired of being miserable, Blossom. I didn't think I'd ever get over Luke, and when I finally summon the courage to try again, Matt rips my heart out and stomps on it."

"I'm a good judge of character. One has to be in my line of work," Blossom said with a chuckle. "I sense that Matt is one of the good guys. I don't believe he'd ever intentionally hurt you. Does he know how you feel about him?"

"No. And I'm not going to tell him." Shelby buried her face in Blossom's bosom and sobbed.

Blossom stroked Shelby's hair until her tears subsided. "You need a break from this B&B," she said, handing Shelby a napkin to dry her eyes. "You've been working hard and worrying about your grandmother. Why don't we go to town for dinner? I have a hankering to try out The Nest."

Shelby pictured them together at the town's most popular hangout—a skinny white girl with an exotic black woman, adorned in a Hawaiian muumuu with a wreath of tropical flowers woven through the spirals of silver curls on her head. Shelby didn't care what anyone thought. After all, she only knew two people her age in town—Matt and her cousin, Harper. But what if Matt took his Hinge date to The Nest?

"Matt won't be there," Blossom said, as though reading her mind.

Shelby didn't ask how Blossom knew this. She seemed to know everything, as though she kept a crystal ball hidden in the deep pockets of her oversized dresses.

"Okay. Let's do it. We can take my car." Shelby jumped to her feet, suddenly eager to drive the new-to-her Jeep Wrangler. Her mother had bought the off-road vehicle, and Shelby had paid to have the exterior painted sky blue and the seats recovered in white upholstery to match Blossom's Heaven Mobile—the small custom bus she referred to as her home away from home.

Blossom rose slowly from the table. "I can hardly wait to ride in the Shelby Cruiser. But first, I need to put away the groceries."

"I'll help you," Shelby said, removing items from the bags while Blossom put them away.

Blossom was placing a carton of milk in the refrigerator when she suddenly froze. "The aura over Magnolia Shores just shifted," she said, turning to face Shelby, her emerald eyes alert. "Danger is lurking in the shadows."

Shelby looked at Blossom as though she'd lost her mind. "What danger? Is there an intruder on the property?"

"I'm not sure. I sense a troublemaker in our midst."

The front door slammed, and a voice called out, "Hello? Is anyone home?"

Shelby deflated. "You are spot on, Blossom. That troublemaker is my sister."

The clicking of high heels preceded Grace's appearance in the kitchen. "There you are. Why didn't you answer me?"

"I didn't hear you," Shelby lied. "Grace, this is Blossom."

Grace's slate-blue eyes narrowed as she gave Blossom a once-over. "Seriously? Your name is Blossom? Are you a flower child or something?"

Blossom let out a belly laugh. "I wish. I would've rocked the hippie era. Unfortunately, I didn't make it to the sixties."

Shelby clamped her hand over her mouth to hide her smile.

"What? I don't get it," Grace said, her eyes darting between Blossom and Shelby.

"It's an inside joke," Shelby said, growing serious. "What're you doing here?"

"I came to see Mom. Since she's obviously not coming home anytime soon. I need help with the wedding. And I wanted to see Izzy of course. I've been so worried about her since the stroke. Can I sleep in my usual room?"

"You can have it for two nights, but you'll have to check out on Wednesday at eleven. We're booked solid through the weekend. The room rate is three hundred and fifty dollars a night," Shelby said with a smirk tugging at her lip.

Grace's jaw hit the floor. "But I'm family."

"That rate already includes the Friends and Family discount." Shelby's hand shot out. "If you give me your credit card, I'll process the charge for you now."

"I'm not paying to stay in my family's home."

Shelby shrugged. "Suit yourself. You can work it out with Pritchard."

"Where's Mom staying?"

"In the cottage with Izzy," Shelby said.

Lines appeared on Grace's forehead. "What cottage?"

Shelby gestured at the window. "That small building across the courtyard—the one we used to think was a garden shed."

Grace's face fell. "Where are you sleeping, Shelby?"

"In a pup tent on the beach. Listening to the waves crashing on the shore is better than my noise machine. I don't even mind when ghost crabs crawl up my pajama pants." Shelby noticed Blossom's body shudder, as though she was struggling to suppress laughter.

"Ugh. You're impossible. I haven't missed you one bit."

Holding her head high, Grace spun on her four-inch heels and glided like a supermodel out of the kitchen.

"Right back at you," Shelby called after her.

Blossom's face turned grave as her emerald eyes followed Grace. "Where does her darkness come from? Certainly not from your sweet mama."

Shelby swiveled her head toward Blossom. "Wait! I thought I was the only person who could see the real Grace. She's a rock star. Everyone adores her, and everything she touches turns to gold."

"Her cloud of negativity is as clear to me as the red dress she's wearing." Wrinkles creased the caramel skin on Blossom's forehead as she stared trancelike down the hallway.

"What're you thinking, Blossom?" Shelby asked.

"I've been waiting to be sent elsewhere for my next assignment, but maybe my elders are keeping me here for a reason."

"I doubt it," Shelby said. "Not even an angel can fix what's wrong with my sister."

"Something tells me my new case has nothing to do with Grace. Maybe another member of your family." Blossom tore her gaze away from the hallway. "I guess time will tell."

"I guess. Let's get out of here before Grace comes back," Shelby said, taking hold of Blossom's hand and dragging her toward the door.

Blossom got into the Jeep's passenger side and inspected the interior. "Girlfriend! I love your new set of wheels," she said, running her hand over the white leather seat.

"Thanks! I'm super excited. I can't wait to drive it on the beach after Labor Day when all the tourists leave." As she navigated the long driveway away from Magnolia Shores, Shelby fiddled with the radio, settling on a country music station. "Pritchard is considering closing the B&B over the winter while The Sanctuary is under construction. He says he'll pay me, but I'm worried I'll be bored out of my mind with nothing to do."

"You're an active girl. You'll need something to occupy your time. Maybe you could get a temporary job at one of the shops or restaurants in town."

Shelby smiled over at her. "That's a brilliant idea, Blossom. Maybe Savannah would hire me as a bartender at The Nest. I could take mixology classes. When The Sanctuary opens, my new skills will come in handy on busy weekends."

Blossom nodded, her curls dancing around on top of her head. "Good thinking!"

At The Nest, Shelby asked for Savannah, but the young hostess shook her head. "She's not here. She went home for dinner. She should be back soon, though. Can I help you?"

"I'm Savannah's niece." Shelby gestured at Blossom. "My friend and I are on a spontaneous outing, and we don't have a reservation. How long is the wait?"

The hostess consulted her iPad. "About forty-five minutes for a table for two. But I have some seats available at the bar."

Shelby looked over at Blossom. "Will your elders get mad if you eat at the bar?"

Blossom chuckled. "They shouldn't, as long as we're eating dinner."

Shelby felt eyes on them as they made their way through the crowded restaurant. Instead of being embarrassed by her eccentric dinner companion, she felt proud to be in the company of such a fantastic woman.

five

· · ·

Grace teetered across the cobblestone courtyard in her high heels. She should've taken the time to change her shoes. Knocking once on the cottage door, she barged in without waiting to be invited. Her mother and grandmother were seated at a small round table playing cards.

Kate looked up in surprise, her mouth agape and card hand pressed against her chest. "Grace! What're you doing here?"

"I need help with wedding stuff. And since you were making no moves to return home, I came to see you." Grace leaned in to kiss her grandmother's cheek. "Izzy, you're looking well," she lied. Her grandmother appeared pale and fragile. Her mother, on the other hand, wore the healthy glow of summer. She studied Kate more closely. There was something different about her mother other than her lightly tanned skin and sun-streaked hair. Had she lost weight? Were the layers in her auburn hair new? Whatever the change, Kate looked years younger.

Turning away from the table, Grace circled the living room. The decor was too country for her taste, although she did find the furnishings cozy. "Why have I never been in this cottage?"

"It was neglected for years, but Harper fixed it up for Izzy after the stroke," Kate said, leaving the table to stand beside Grace.

"Who's Harper?" Grace asked.

Kate rammed her elbow into Grace's side. "Your cousin. Remember, you met her at Pritchard and Savannah's wedding? She's their daughter."

"Right. The bastard child."

"Don't be crude, Grace. And Harper is their legitimate child."

Grace noticed a frumpy woman seated across the room in a rocking chair. "I'm Grace. And you are?"

The woman lifted a hand in a wave. "Jackie, your gramma's caregiver."

"Oh. Right." Grace turned to her mother. "Is there any food around here? I'm starving?"

"Sure. Let's go over to the main house so Izzy can rest. We can talk about the wedding while we eat." Kate smiled at Jackie. "I picked up a rotisserie chicken for Mom's dinner, and there's fresh fruit and a Greek salad in the fridge."

Jackie waved them on. "Don't worry about us. We'll be fine."

Kate and Grace walked arm in arm across the courtyard. "This is such a pleasant surprise. I'm so glad to see you. Does Shelby know you're here? She'll need to assign you to a room."

"I saw her. She's charging me three hundred and fifty bucks a night for the room I used to stay in for free."

Kate chuckled. "As you can see, things have changed around here. I'll work something out with Pritchard."

They entered the house through the front door. "I'll meet you in the kitchen in a few minutes," Grace said, dragging her suitcase up the stairs to her room. She changed into more comfortable clothes, grabbed her laptop and the tote bag containing her wedding planning materials, and hurried back down the stairs.

Grace peered over her mother's shoulder as she removed salad ingredients from the refrigerator. "We should celebrate. Do you have any Champagne?"

"What're we celebrating?"

Grace shrugged. "Life. My wedding. My arrival at Magnolia Shores."

Kate searched the shelves. "I'm sorry, sweetheart. I don't even think we have any wine." She opened the freezer drawer and removed a bottle of citron vodka. "We have this. And there's some club soda in the pantry."

"I guess that'll have to do," Grace said, locating the soda and mixing her drink.

She sipped her cocktail while watching Kate make a salad of grilled chicken, goat's cheese, and mixed berries. While they ate, Grace shared her new ideas for the reception—a professional fireworks display, getaway helicopter, and a crystal chandelier for the tent.

"That sounds lovely, sweetheart, but we don't have room in the budget for such extravagant extras."

"Why not? We can afford it," Grace said, stabbing a slice of grilled chicken with her fork."

"That doesn't mean we should throw away money. We need to adhere to your father's generous budget."

Grace cringed at the mention of her father. She wondered if he and Claudia were having a sleepover tonight.

The rumble of a loud car engine sounded in the courtyard. Minutes later, Shelby and Blossom came through the back door with a little dog running alongside them. The dog skidded to a halt at Grace's feet and growled at her.

"Make it stop," Grace said, kicking at it with her flip-flop.

"Jolene is harmless," Blossom said, scooping up the dog. "She had the same reaction to Izzy when they first met. She's overly protective. She just needs to get to know you."

"Guess what we brought you, Mama," Shelby said, dangling a plastic grocery bag in front of Kate.

Since when did Shelby call Kate Mama? Kate thought. *South Carolina is turning her sister into the sweetest little Southern belle. Gag.*

"Is that what I think it is?" Kate asked, eyeing the bag.

"Yep." Shelby removed a pint of gelato from the bag. "And

they had your favorite flavor—strawberry shortcake." She retrieved a stack of bowls from the cabinet. "Do you want some, Grace?"

"No, thanks. I'm on a diet. I'm getting married soon."

"Your wedding is eight months away. You could gain and lose ten pounds by then." Shelby scooped ice cream into three bowls, placing one in front of Kate.

Grace wagged a finger at Kate. "That's it! I've been trying to figure out what's different about you. You've gained weight since you've been in the Lowcountry."

Kate squirmed uncomfortably in her seat. "I may have put on a few pounds. I've been eating Blossom's amazing cooking."

Shelby smiled adoringly at their mother as she handed Kate a spoon. "Mama has reverted to her roots. She's a wholesome Carolina girl again with sun-kissed skin, freckles, and padded curves."

Grace glared at her sister. "Stop already, Shelby. *Mama* is so redneck."

"You're in South Carolina now, Grace. If you don't like it, leave." Shelby moved her chair so close to Kate that she was practically sitting on her lap. She recapped her dinner at The Nest, speaking to Kate like no one else was in the room. Kate and Shelby had developed a close bond during their time here together. And Grace didn't like it one bit. Grace was the golden child, the apple of her mother's eye. She would not tolerate Shelby moving in on her territory.

Grace sat back in her chair, arms folded over her chest. "So, Shelby . . . Great job of breaking up Luke and Alexis. What's the big deal? You can't have him, so you don't want anyone else to?"

Shelby sunk her spoon into her gelato. "Luke came to see me, looking for some side action. Alexis deserves to know what her fiancé was up to. I figured she wouldn't believe me, so I posted the pic on Instagram instead."

"What's the big deal?" Grace asked. "Everyone cheats these days. You didn't have to ruin his life."

Shelby's eyes widened. "Are you saying you wouldn't mind if Wyatt cheated on you?"

"Wyatt would never cheat on me," Grace said as a searing pain wrenched her gut. She never thought her father would cheat on her mother either.

Grace looked from her sister to their mother. "Have any of your friends' husbands cheated on them?"

"A few, but they all got divorced," Kate said. "I don't know many people who would put up with that kind of betrayal. What's the point of getting married if you're going to sleep with someone else?"

"Exactly." Blossom's spoon clanked against the sides of the bowl as she scraped up the last of the gelato. "Trust is the cornerstone of any relationship, the solid ground upon which all else is built. When infidelity occurs, it cracks this foundation, leaving it susceptible to even the smallest disturbances. Repairing such fundamental damage is a daunting, often insurmountable challenge."

Grace gawked. *Who is this weirdo?* Blossom sounded like a minister preaching to her congregation.

Kate smiled softly. "Well said, Blossom."

Shelby pushed back from the table. "That's so profound, I need to be alone to think about it. I'm going to my room."

"Wait for me, and I'll walk with you." Blossom gathered the ice cream bowls, rinsed them in the sink, and placed them in the dishwasher.

Kate watched Shelby and Blossom file out the back door with the dog on their heels. "What's with that odd woman?" Grace asked.

"Blossom takes a little getting used to, but she's . . . There is no way to describe her. She's just Blossom." Kate smiled across the table at Grace. "I still can't believe you're here. How long are you planning to stay?"

Grace chewed on her lip as she pondered her return home. She hadn't been to Magnolia Shores in years and could use a few days to decompress. She had nothing pressing at work. "I'd like to stay longer, but Shelby's kicking me out on Wednesday. Apparently, the B&B is booked for the weekend."

"My room in the cottage has an extra twin bed. You can bunk with me if you can handle Izzy's snoring."

"I can handle it. Her snoring can't be worse than Wyatt's. I probably have an extra set of earplugs in my cosmetics bag." *Bunking* in a twin bed with her mother and grandmother was not Grace's cup of tea. Maybe she would borrow her sister's pup tent.

Kate got up from the table. "If you stay through the weekend, we can fly home together on Sunday. I'll book our tickets."

Grace stood to face her. "That sounds perfect. Why don't we go to the Sandy Island Club in the morning? We could play tennis and have lunch."

Kate laughed. "Lunch, yes! Tennis, no! I haven't played in years."

"So what? It'll be fun."

"Let's see if we can get a court first. Good night, sweetheart." Kate cupped her daughter's face, thumbing her cheek, before disappearing out the back door.

Grace turned out the lights and made her way upstairs to her room. She threw open the French doors and stepped onto the small balcony, inhaling deep breaths of the salty air. Hearing the ocean waves crash against the shore in the distance eased the tension in her body. She'd made the right decision to prolong her departure. She needed some time to herself. Being at Magnolia Shores always helped put her life into perspective. Her encounter with Claudia seemed light years away. She wanted the image of that woman in her mother's robe out of her head. If she tried really hard, maybe she could forget about it altogether.

six

· · ·

Darkness had set in by the time Kate left the main house. Her mind reeled, and she needed time alone to collect herself. Grabbing her laptop and sketch pad from the cottage, she went to the pool. She didn't think it fair to compare her daughters, given their vastly different personalities. But after spending weeks with easygoing Shelby, she was starkly reminded of how dramatic Grace could be about practically everything. What planet was Grace living on? The idea of leaving a wedding reception in a helicopter was preposterous.

Kate stretched out on a lounge chair and opened her computer. She checked for the lowest fare and booked two seats on American Airlines departing from Charleston midmorning on Sunday. The thought of returning to her empty life in Austin unsettled her. When had she begun to think of her life as empty? Part of it was her job. She no longer found *selling* fixtures challenging. She yearned to be on the creative side of the industry. As for her marriage, she and Rand had grown further apart over the past few years. They were far from the point of no return, but if they wanted their marriage to work, they needed to address their issues instead of ignoring them.

She placed her laptop on the chair beside her and picked up

her sketch pad. The dim light from the landscape fixtures cast a soft glow over the design she'd been working on—a navy lacquered pendant with brass accent finishings.

Kate was so engrossed in her work that she was startled by a man's voice. "You okay out here by yourself?"

She looked up to find Silas looming over her. He wore many hats at the B&B—maintenance man, bellhop, and security guard. "I'm fine, but thanks for checking on me."

Silas gave her a curt nod. "I'm just making my nightly rounds," he said, directing the beam of his flashlight at her sketch pad. "So, you're an artist?"

"I'm a lighting consultant. Drawing fixtures is a hobby."

"Can I see? I know a little about interior design."

Kate hugged the sketchbook to her chest. She was not ready to show anyone her designs, let alone a practical stranger. "You don't strike me as the decorator type."

Silas chuckled. "I know a little about a lot of things. I was incarcerated for ten years at the Ridgeland Correctional Institution. I spent every free moment in the library, reading everything I could get my hands on."

Kate sat up straighter in her chair. "Wait. You were in prison? For what crime, if you don't mind me asking?"

"I don't mind." He gestured at the lounge chair beside her. "May I?"

"Of course. Help yourself."

He lowered his tall frame to the chair. "My ex-wife accused me of aggravated assault to protect her boyfriend. After serving ten years of a twenty-five-year sentence, my ex admitted she had lied about the incident. Two weeks after I was released from prison, that same boyfriend, whom she had married while I was in prison, murdered her."

Kate's breath hitched as her hand flew to her mouth. "Silas! That's awful. I'm so sorry."

"Thanks. I'm grateful to Pritchard for giving me this job. Your mother doesn't know I was in prison, which is probably for the best."

Kate pretended to lock her lips and throw away the key. "I won't say a word." She studied the tattoos covering his muscular arms—sayings, a clock with no hands, and barbed wire across his right bicep. "Did you get those in prison?"

"Most of them. Tattoos tell a person's life story inside and outside prison." His eyes traveled back to her sketch pad. "Visual Comfort and Hudson Valley are among my favorite lighting brands."

"Mine too. I'm impressed. You *do* know your stuff." She pulled the sketchbook away from her chest. "I'll let you see them if you promise not to laugh."

"Why would I laugh?" Setting down his flashlight, he took the pad from her and flipped through the pages. "These are excellent, Kate. I mean, seriously good."

Pride swelled in her chest. "Thank you. You're the first person I've ever shown them to."

"I'm honored." Starting at the beginning, he turned the pages a second time. "Have you considered producing them?"

Considered? She thought of little else. "I have a friend at Crescent Moon Lighting in Charleston. Do you know them?"

"Yes! Another one of my favorites."

"Joan and I have been working together for years, but we've never met in person. I've been thinking of paying her a visit while I'm here. Maybe I'll show her my designs."

"You totally should! Your designs would be a great fit for their brand," he said, closing the sketchbook and handing it back to her. "I met your other daughter earlier. She seems . . ." He paused as though considering the right word. "*Different* than Shelby."

"That's an understatement. They are nothing alike. And they don't get along, which makes family events difficult. If only they would try to be cordial to each other. But they are both as stubborn as the day is long." Kate massaged her temples. "I wasn't expecting Grace. She showed up out of the blue. She needs my help planning her wedding, and I've been neglecting her. I should've gone home weeks ago." She smiled up at him. "I don't mean to dump my problems in your lap."

"You're not dumping on me. I *asked* about Grace." His dark eyes warmed. "You have no reason to feel guilty, Kate. Your mother had a stroke. She needed you. Grace strikes me as perfectly capable of planning her own wedding."

"She can handle everything except paying for it," Kate said, realizing the truth in her words as they left her mouth. Grace didn't need Kate. She needed her credit card.

Silas stood to go. "I should finish my rounds."

Kate's heart sank. She enjoyed his company. Maybe a little too much. She missed the companionship of a man. Even when she and Rand were together, her husband's thoughts were a million miles away. "Thanks for critiquing my designs," she said, smoothing her hand over her sketchbook cover.

"Anytime. They're exceptional. You should totally connect with your friend at Crescent Moon."

Kate reached for her laptop. "I'm going to email her right now while I have the guts."

"Good for you! Let me know what she says." Silas shined his flashlight around the pool. "Are you sure you're okay here by yourself?"

"Positive. Remember, I grew up at Magnolia Shores. I often sat by the pool at night when I needed to think."

"Unfortunately, that safe world has changed. We have to be aware of our surroundings at all times."

She smiled up at him. "I think we're fine as long as we have Blossom looking out for us."

Silas laughed. "True." He circled the pool, then crossed the terrace in front of the house, disappearing into the darkness.

Kate typed out a message to Joan at Crescent Moon Lighting, explaining that she was in the Lowcountry and would like to meet for coffee or lunch one day this week. She pressed Send and immediately second-guessed herself. Was she ready for such a drastic move?

Kate's drawings were among the few sources of joy left in her life. If Joan didn't approve of them, her hopes for a design career would be crushed. On the other hand, Silas had praised them as exceptional. What if Joan thought so too? This could be the beginning of a new career path for Kate. And it couldn't come at a moment too soon.

Joan's response was waiting in Kate's inbox when she woke on Tuesday morning. She would love to meet in person and invited Kate for coffee on Wednesday morning at nine. Kate considered the trip to Charleston. She would need to leave no later than eight. With so few guests currently in the house, she didn't feel guilty asking Blossom to cover the breakfast shift for her.

Kate's stomach churned. Once she shared her drawings, Joan would assess her talent, sealing her fate. Was she prepared to walk away from her passion if Joan disapproved of her designs? She'd find out tomorrow. But today, she had a tennis date with Grace.

Grace tortured Kate on the tennis court. She gasped for air as she attempted to chase down her daughter's winning shots. She even thought she might faint in the midsummer heat. She'd let herself get out of shape. She couldn't remember the last time she exerted herself. Her twice-weekly barre classes weren't cutting it.

When Grace defeated her 6-0 in the first set, Kate's clothes were soaked through with sweat.

"Wanna go another set?" Grace asked with a self-satisfied smirk on her lips.

"Not hardly." Kate checked her watch. "We have just enough time to shower and dress before our noon lunch reservation."

They gathered their belongings and headed to the locker room. "I don't remember this club being so run down," Grace said, complaining the entire time they were getting ready. The towels were rough, the water smelled like rust, and the shampoo flattened her hair. By the time they sat down at their table on the club's terrace, Kate was wondering how she had raised such a bratty snob.

"So, Mom . . . I think I've found my dress." Grace removed a folded magazine advertisement from her purse. "We'll have to fly to New York. Isabella Blanc is the designer, and it's available exclusively through her studio. We could make a weekend of it. We could see a Broadway show, eat in fabulous restaurants, and shop to our heart's content. Isn't it gorgeous?" she said, unfolding the glossy page and handing it to Kate.

The dress was indeed gorgeous—strapless with a simple bodice and a mile-long train of ivory satin. "It's stunning. Do we have any idea how much it cost?"

Grace pulled out her phone, accessed the gown on Isabella Blanc's website, and handed the phone to Kate. The price of the dress was triple what they had budgeted. "Keep looking, Grace," she said, returning the phone to her daughter.

Grace pouted her lower lip. "Please, Mom. We can afford it."

"That's beside the point. Your father has established a budget for a reason. You can find something equally elegant for a fraction of the cost."

Grace stared longingly at the dress. "Why does Dad get to make all the rules? I will never let Wyatt control me like that. You have family money. Not Dad. You could buy this dress for me if you wanted to," she said, waving the magazine ad at Kate.

Kate frowned. "Why do I get the feeling we're discussing more than your wedding dress?"

"Because maybe I am," Grace said, neatly folding the paper and slipping it back inside her purse. "You're accomplished and beautiful, and you have a wonderful personality. You could be an independent modern woman, but you let him treat you like his servant."

Kate choked on her sweet tea. "That's not true!" she said, although maybe it was a little true. Kate avoided conflict. Going along with Rand was easier than arguing. But she'd been going along with him for so long she'd lost sight of her own interests.

Grace arched an eyebrow. "Oh, yeah? When's the last time you did anything for yourself?"

Kate swept an arm at her surroundings. "I'm here, aren't I?"

"Be real, Mom. You're here for Izzy."

That she'd come for Izzy was true, but she'd stayed because she couldn't bring herself to go home. "There are several bridal boutiques in Charleston. I'm meeting with a lighting designer in the morning. You could shop while I'm in my meeting, and then we could visit the bridal boutiques afterward."

Grace let out an indignant huff. "No way! I refuse to dress like a Southern belle on my wedding day. Maybe we can go to Dallas when we get home?"

"That sounds like an acceptable compromise," Kate said with a curt nod. She grew silent as she perused the menu. When had she relinquished control of her life to Rand? On their wedding day? During these past weeks, she'd felt the independent, carefree girl she'd been in her youth reemerging. The taste of freedom was as exhilarating as the salty air. But was she willing to make the sacrifices to get it? Her marriage. Her life and beautiful home in Austin. Truth be told, with her girls gone, that house no longer felt like a home. She had many happy memories of raising her family there. But *home* for Kate would always be Magnolia Shores.

seven

. . .

S helby was mixing up her first experimental cocktail in the kitchen when Izzy shuffled in with her rollator and a caregiver on her heels.

"There you are. I've been looking for you." Izzy eyed the mess scattered across the counter—sliced peaches, fresh mint leaves, and open bottles of elderflower liqueur and Champagne. "Too early in the day for drinking," she said with a chuckle. While her grandmother's sentences were still broken, Izzy's speech was the clearest it had been since her stroke.

"I'm studying mixology," Shelby said, adding a cup of sweet tea to the pitcher. She'd stayed up late researching mixology online. Knowing how to mix drinks with fresh juices and herbs would serve her well in many aspects of her job.

"Since when?" Izzy asked in a suspicious tone.

"Since yesterday. It's my new hobby." Because Shelby wasn't sure how much Izzy knew about construction plans for The Sanctuary, she decided not to mention Pritchard's intention to close the B&B over the winter. "I'm creating a welcome drink for our guests. I think I'll call it Peach Tea Porch Sipper. Here, try some." Pouring a splash into three glasses, she handed one to Izzy and another to the caregiver, keeping the third for herself.

The caregiver swallowed the liquid in one gulp. "Delicious."

Izzy took a sip. "Tasty." She smacked her lips. "Needs some lemon juice."

Shelby curled her lip. "Lemon juice?"

"Yes. Lemon juice to go with sweet tea."

"That makes sense. I'll try it." Retrieving a bottle of lemon juice from the refrigerator, Shelby added a squirt to her glass and tasted the concoction again. "Yum. You were right. The lemon juice makes a huge difference." She drained the rest of the punch. "I'll offer it to our guests when they arrive tomorrow."

"I need to sit a spell," Izzy said, pushing her walker out of the way and dropping down to a chair at the table. She motioned Shelby to the table. "Join me. Need to talk to you about something."

Shelby's antenna popped up at her grandmother's serious tone. She hoped Izzy wasn't having more medical problems. She pulled a chair up to the table beside her grandmother. "What's up, Izzy? I hope nothing's wrong."

"Not at all. I need a favor." She dug a folded sheet of her embossed stationery out of the pocket of her linen slacks. "Family coming for dinner. I need you to read this for me."

Shelby read the letter addressed to Pritchard, Savannah, and Harper. Her heartfelt words expressed her sorrow for interfering in Pritchard and Savannah's relationship thirty years ago, causing them to lose their baby, Harper. As tears filled her eyes, Shelby released the letter, letting it float to the table. "I'd be honored to help you. When would you like me to read it? Maybe when everyone arrives, to get it out of the way before dinner?"

Izzy nodded. "That would be best."

An idea struck Shelby. "Hey! Do you want me to make a special drink for the occasion?"

Izzy gave her a crooked smile. "Sure! Call it *The Apology*."

Shelby bolted out of her chair. "I'll get started on it right away."

Shelby was waiting in the foyer for Pritchard's family to arrive when her sister came gliding down the stairs.

"Shelby! What're you doing standing here alone? Did you lose your best friend? Oh, wait. I forgot you don't have any friends."

"Buzz off, Grace!"

Shelby heard voices outside and opened the door for Pritchard, Savannah, and Harper. They were surprised to see Grace and welcomed her with hugs and kisses.

"Izzy would like to speak with you before dinner. She's waiting with Mama in Edward's study," Shelby said, motioning them to the living room.

When Grace stepped in line behind them, Shelby grabbed her arm. "Sorry, but you're not invited."

Grace planted her hands on her hips. "Why not?"

"This matter doesn't concern you," Shelby said, entering her grandfather's study and closing the door in her sister's face.

Pritchard, Savannah, and Harper sat together on the small sofa while Kate and Izzy occupied the wingback chairs. Shelby stood between them.

"Izzy asked me to read a letter she wrote to you. She would read it herself if she weren't still struggling with her speech." Shelby unfolded the letter and began to read. "After my stroke, when I was still unconscious, I encountered your father, my beloved husband. We'll call it a dream, although it felt so real, like a visitation. I was at the doorstep of heaven, the sense of peace enveloping me like a warm blanket. But Edward wouldn't let me go with him. I have unfinished business here, on earth, with you. You may remember that I was trying to tell you something important when I had the stroke."

When Shelby hesitated, Izzy nodded for her to continue.

"I'm going to stop for a minute to pass around these Champagne flutes, and then I'll continue with Izzy's letter."

Shelby said, retrieving a tray of stemless Champagne flutes from the desk and passing it around the room.

Savannah sniffed the orange-colored concoction. "This is a pretty drink. What is it?"

Shelby smiled. "Just a little something I mixed up." Returning the tray to the desk, she lowered herself to the arm of her grandmother's chair. "Now, Izzy would like to say something to you."

With her right hand pressed to her chest, Izzy lifted her Champagne flute with her left. "From the bottom of my heart, I am . . ."—tears filled her eyes— "so truly . . . sorry."

Not a dry eye was in the room as they clinked glasses.

"There's more in the letter," Shelby said and waited for everyone to settle before continuing. "My actions drastically altered your lives, and I'm ashamed of the way I treated you when you came back into Pritchard's life. I was too bullheaded to realize I wasn't losing Pritchard, I was gaining a granddaughter and daughter-in-law. While I can never give you back the time you lost, I'm grateful for the opportunity to make things right with you. I love you all, and I intend to live out my last days making amends. I would be eternally grateful if you could find it in your hearts to give me another chance."

The others rose and huddled around Izzy, hugging and kissing her.

Shelby held up her glass. "Here's to starting over."

"Here, here," the small group called out in unison.

Harper sipped her drink. "This is delicious."

Shelby smiled at her grandmother. "We named it The Apology."

Savannah took a drink and licked her lips. "It's very light and citrusy and clean. I'm impressed, Shelby. If you decide to take up bartending, let me know."

Shelby laughed. Now was not the time to tell her aunt she might be looking for a part-time job over the winter. As the family lingered, the tension that had plagued its members for so long was replaced by a feeling of hopefulness for the future. When the others migrated outside to the terrace with their cocktails, Shelby went to the kitchen to help Blossom prepare dinner.

Blossom looked up from basting the baby back ribs with barbeque sauce. "Well? How did it go?"

"I think it went well. Pritchard, Savannah, and Harper seemed to need to hear her apology as much as Izzy needed to say it."

"Excellent. I hope they can finally put that unpleasant business behind them," Blossom said and returned to basting.

"What can I do to help?" Shelby asked.

"Well, let's see." Blossom brushed a stray curl off her forehead with the back of her hand. "The table is set. The ribs have been cooking all day in the oven on low. I just need to finish them on the grill. You can get the cornbread salad and platter of tomatoes out of the refrigerator. Oh, and we need to pour tea in the glasses on the table."

"I'm on it." Shelby removed the items from the refrigerator and took the pitcher of sweet tea outside to the table.

She was filling the glasses when Harper wandered over. As always, she looked amazing in a black knit sundress, her white-blonde hair pulled back in a perky ponytail.

"Your sister is asking a lot of questions about my relationship with Savannah and Pritchard," Harper said, handing Shelby a glass.

Shelby filled the glass and handed it back to her. "Be careful what you tell her. She's not trustworthy, and she doesn't need to know your business."

"Thanks for the warning." Moving on to the next place setting, Harper asked, "How are things going with Matt?"

"Not great," Shelby said without looking up from pouring tea. "He had a date with a girl he met on Hinge."

"I was wondering about that. I ran into them at Clam and Claw."

Shelby set down the pitcher. "Really? What's she like?"

Harper's face flushed. "Hard to say. I only saw her from a distance."

Shelby frowned. "So, she's pretty."

"I guess," Harper said with a shrug. "But since you and Matt aren't exclusive, I wondered if you'd be willing to go on a blind date. I'm dying to set you up with Cody's friend, Josh Morgan. He's a super nice guy and extremely attractive. He comes from a good family and has an adorable personality: friendly and outgoing with a great sense of humor."

"If he's so wonderful, why doesn't he have a girlfriend?"

"I don't know. I guess he hasn't found the right girl yet."

Shelby narrowed her teal eyes. "What aren't you telling me, Harper?"

"His career choice might be a deal-breaker for you. I know you're looking for someone in a more prestigious profession, like a doctor or lawyer. Josh owns his own landscaping company."

"Actually, I've changed my mind about guys and their careers. I've decided I prefer the outdoorsy type. But I'm taking some time for myself. I'm not ready to date yet." Shelby cradled the tea pitcher as she walked back toward the house.

Harper trailed her to the kitchen. "The Catawba Music Festival is this weekend featuring a diverse lineup of bands—country, classic rock, and reggae. The opening event is Thursday night. Our friend group is going. It'll be a casual date. You can ride with Cody and me, and we'll meet Josh at the party. If nothing else, this will give you a chance to meet some other local kids."

Shelby worshipped her cousin. She would not pass up the opportunity to spend time with Harper. And the bluegrass festival sounded like fun. "Why not? As long as we keep it casual."

Harper drew an X over her chest. "Cross my heart. No strings attached. But I think you'll like him. And you two would make a cute couple."

Shelby laughed. "You're getting ahead of yourself." She handed her cousin the bowl of cornbread salad. "Do you mind taking this out to the table? I'm right behind you with the tomatoes."

Shelby sprinkled feta cheese on the tomatoes and drizzled balsamic dressing over the top. She wanted to be a couple with Matt. But since he's currently dating Hinge Girl, she might as well have some fun.

eight

· · ·

When Joan arrived, Kate was already seated at a table in the La Pâtisserie at the Hotel Bennett. She was prettier in person than her profile picture on the Crescent Moon Lighting website. The women chatted about industry trends over cappuccinos. Realizing her time was running out, Kate summoned the nerve to show Joan her designs and she appeared genuinely impressed. She flipped through the pages of the sketchbook and then started over from the beginning, studying the drawings more closely her second time through.

She closed the sketchbook, sliding it back across the table to Kate. "These are exceptional, Kate. How long have you been designing?"

"For years. It happened by accident, actually. As a lighting expert, I've developed a keen understanding of what my clients are looking for in fixtures. I combined that knowledge with my long-time hobby of drawing, and now I have this portfolio."

"Have you considered producing them?" Joan asked.

"That's why I'm showing them to you. I have more sketchbooks with a wide variety of styles at home. My designs have taken on nautical elements during my recent extended stay in the Lowcountry. I thought they might be a good fit for Crescent Moon."

Joan pressed her lips thin. "We could potentially buy a couple of your designs, but we're not in a position to take on a new brand."

Kate's heart sank. "I understand. Unfortunately, I'm not interested in selling my designs piecemeal."

Joan sat back in her chair, sipping her cappuccino. "You might reach out to Ethan Blake for advice. He was once the most skilled craftsman in the industry. He comes from a long line of artisans, and his work was top quality."

"Is he no longer in the industry?"

"He worked for Crescent Moon for years. However, he had some personal issues relating to his homosexuality. We had to let him go when he started abusing alcohol." She rummaged through her purse for her phone. "Last I heard, he was working at his partner's interior design firm in Beaufort." She thumbed her phone's screen. "I just sent you his contact information."

Kate's phone pinged in her purse with the incoming text. "Thank you. I'll reach out to him right away. I value your opinion, Joan. You have excellent style, and you know the market better than anyone. What would you do in my shoes?"

Joan set down her mug and looked through Kate's sketches one last time. Closing the sketchbook, she leaned across the table and lowered her voice. "You have the potential to become a serious competitor for Crescent Moon. I see the excitement in your eyes, and I have a hunch there's no stopping you. As a friend, I say go for it. When you run us out of business, you must promise to give me a job."

Kate laughed. "You've got it. I appreciate your honesty." Suddenly eager to talk to Ethan, she gathered her belongings and stood to go. "Thanks for meeting with me, Joan."

Joan pressed her cheek against Kate's. "Good luck and stay in touch."

Kate waited until she had crossed the Ashley River, heading

south toward Water's Edge, before clicking on Ethan Blake's contact information. When he didn't answer, she left a detailed message explaining that Joan had recommended Kate reach out to him regarding starting her own lighting company.

She dropped the phone in her lap as the words echoed in her mind. *Her own lighting company, her dream come true. Was this really happening?*

Her phone vibrated in her lap five minutes later with Ethan's return call. She'd expected a middle-aged man, but he sounded much younger, in his thirties if she had to guess.

Ethan asked about Joan's well-being and briefly explained his reason for leaving Crescent Lighting. "My parents were devastated when I came out of the closet, and I was going through a rough patch. They've finally accepted that I'm gay, and they love Jared, my partner. Normally, I wouldn't share such personal information with a stranger, but I wanted you to understand why I left Crescent."

"I can't imagine how difficult that must have been for you. Are you still working as an interior designer?"

"I am, and I love it. Jared and I have built a thriving business. But I miss working with my hands. I've been considering venturing out on my own as well. Maybe we should join forces. I'd love to meet in person. I'm tied up for most of the day. Is there any chance you could meet tomorrow afternoon around five o'clock?"

Excitement flickered across Kate's chest. "Yes! I'll come to you."

"Great! We can meet in my shop. I'll text you my address."

Kate hung up with Ethan and called her best friend.

Claudia answered in a panicked voice. "Kate! What's wrong?"

"Nothing's wrong. Can't a woman call her best friend?"

Claudia laughed awkwardly. "Yes, of course. I just haven't heard from you in weeks."

"Sorry. I've been busy with Mom. Do you still have a key to my house?"

"Um . . . Yes. Why?"

Kate's skin prickled. Why did her friend sound so suspicious? "Because I need a favor. There are some sketchbooks in the bottom left drawer of my desk in the kitchen. Is there any chance you could overnight them to me?"

Claudia sighed as though relieved. "I guess."

Kate frowned. "You sound funny, Claudia. Is everything all right?"

"Oh, sure. I'm just reading some emails. But I can run over to your house now. Text me your address in South Carolina, and I'll get those out right away."

As she ended the call, Kate had a strange feeling Claudia was hiding something. Her best friend didn't work and had a full-time housekeeper. Now that her children were grown, Claudia had little to occupy her time and often complained about boredom. Something besides emails was distracting her.

nine

· · ·

A work emergency occupied Grace on her laptop for most of the morning. She'd ignored the housekeeper's requests for her to vacate the room until someone pounded on the door. "Security! Open up!" a menacing voice demanded.

"Go away! I'm on a business call," she yelled back.

"This is your last warning, Miss St. Clair. If you don't vacate the room, I'll call the police."

"Hold your horses. I'm coming." She strode across the room and swung open the door to find the tattooed bellman standing in the hallway. "What's the big deal? Why can't I stay?"

"Checkout time was eleven o'clock. Guests have reserved this room for the weekend. Housekeeping needs to clean before check-in starts at four."

Grace checked her phone for the time. It was already three o'clock. "I didn't realize it was so late. I've been working all morning. Give me a few minutes to gather my things," she said and slammed the door in his face.

She packed her belongings and wheeled her suitcase across the bumpy cobblestone courtyard. Entering the cottage, she called out, "Yoo-hoo. Is anyone home?"

Her grandmother's bedroom door was closed. Assuming Izzy

was napping, she tiptoed to her mother's room, leaving her suitcase at the door while she inspected her new accommodations. The mattress was too firm for her liking, there was no room in the tiny closet for her clothes, and a palmetto tree obstructed the window view of Catawba Sound. When sounds that made her want to vomit came through the closed bathroom door, she ran out of the cottage and back across the courtyard to the pool. Grabbing a beach chair, she continued down the path through the dunes.

Grace unfolded her chair at the edge of the surf and dug her toes into the wet sand. She searched for flights to Austin on her phone, but they were all too expensive without advance notice. She wasn't ready to leave yet, anyway. Leaning her head back, she closed her eyes and listened to the sound of waves crashing. She remembered what her sister had said about sleeping on the beach. Shelby's pup tent would be better than sharing the cottage with her mother and grandmother. She shivered, remembering the sounds she'd heard coming from the bathroom.

Grace got up, collapsed her chair, and retraced her steps back up to the house. She found her sister at the reception desk, checking in two new arrivals. She stood at the desk next to the couple, shifting her weight while folding and unfolding her arms. Failing to get her sister's attention, Grace loudly cleared her throat.

Shelby avoided eye contact with Grace, gesturing with her finger that she would be with her in a minute.

Grace rolled her eyes and let out a loud huff. Stepping back from the desk, she studied the new guests. The man's face was set in an angry scowl, and the woman's eyes were swollen as though she'd been crying.

Shelby swiped their credit card, printed off a receipt, and handed them a room key. "Would you care for a welcome cocktail?"

The man gave a nonchalant shrug, and the woman bobbed her head. "Yes! Please!"

Shelby got up from the desk and entered Edward's study, returning with two clear plastic cups filled with rum punch. "Silas will help you with your bags," she said, handing the couple the drinks.

Shelby watched the couple head up the stairs before turning her attention to Grace. "Can I help you with something?"

"Silas kicked me out of my room. You need to give me your pup tent."

Bewilderment crossed her sister's face, followed closely by disbelief. "God, you're gullible. I can't believe you actually thought I was sleeping in a pup tent."

A flash of anger made Grace's vision turn red. "Where are you staying then?"

"In a tiny room on the second floor of the pool house," Shelby said, returning to her seat behind the desk.

"I'll pay you a hundred bucks a night for your room," Grace said, removing her wallet from her purse and handing Shelby a wad of folded twenties.

Shelby cocked an eyebrow. "And where am I supposed to stay?"

"In the cottage with Mom. As the reservationist, you're obligated to find me suitable accommodations."

"I'm not obligated to you for anything, Grace. I'm sure you can find a suitable pup tent at Coastal Hardware."

"Okay, two hundred dollars. But that's my final offer," Grace said, digging more twenties out of her wallet.

"My room isn't available for rent, Grace," Shelby said, sitting down in her chair.

"You're such a little twit, Shelby. No wonder Luke broke up with you. There's no way you and I are related. Mom and Dad must have adopted you."

Shelby was back on her feet, bending forward and planting her hands on the desk. "Is that so? Then explain why I look just like Mom. You, on the other hand, don't resemble either of our parents. Maybe you're the one who was adopted."

Grace dove across the desk, plowing into Shelby. They crashed against the wall and sank to the floor, a heap of swinging fists, hair pulling, and fingernail clawing. Their uncle's loud voice demanding they break it up didn't deter them. Grace pulled herself on top of Shelby, straddling her and slapping her face repeatedly. Shelby reached for her sister's throat, longing to choke her, but her arms were too short.

Over her sister's shoulder, she watched Silas hook an arm around Grace's midsection and drag her, feet kicking and arms flailing, away from the desk.

Prichard helped Shelby to her feet. "Are you all right? What on earth has gotten into you two?" He pointed at the front door. "We have guests arriving, waiting to check in. They can hear you outside in the courtyard."

"I . . . um . . ." Shelby didn't know how to respond. Throwing Grace under the bus would make her appear childish. Besides, Shelby shared the blame. She'd badgered Grace into attacking her. Damn her sister. She'd worked so hard to impress her uncle, and now Grace would get her fired from a job she loved.

When her mother appeared in the doorway, hot tears sprang to her eyes. "Cover for me, please," Shelby said, brushing past Kate. She caught a glimpse of herself in the mirror as she fled the foyer. Her hair was wild, blood seeped from the scratches on her face, and her tears traced angry paths down her cheeks.

Shelby stormed across the courtyard, past the cottage, and out to the dock. She was having a one-sided tirade with Grace, unleashing every curse word she knew at her sister when Matt pulled up in his boat. She stepped onto his boat before he reached the dock. "Get me out of here before I murder my sister."

"Yes, ma'am," he said, throwing the boat in reverse. When they were safely away from the dock, he rammed the throttle forward and sped off around the tip of the island. She stood beside him, gripping the console's railing, as he navigated the boat across the ocean swells.

They were a quarter mile offshore when he finally slowed. "Is this far enough?"

Shelby glanced behind them at her grandmother's house, barely visible from the distance. "It works." She noticed Matt for the first time, his shirt clinging to his abs and the salt from the sea making his hair gleam in the sunlight. She could no longer hide her attraction to him. She wrapped an arm around his neck and pressed her lips to his, unbuttoning his shorts.

"Are you sure about this?" Matt asked, breathless, his mouth hovering near hers.

"I'm positive. I need this right now."

"Okay. If you say so."

As they fumbled with their clothes, Matt dropped to his knees, pulling her to the boat's floor with him. Their bodies melded as though they'd done this many times before. Grace's orgasm shook her to the core, the release more about her inner turmoil than her interaction with Matt.

Afterward, as they lay with their limbs entwined on the bottom of the boat, Matt said, "I should cry rape, except that was totally hot."

"I'm sorry, Matt. I was so angry at my sister. I felt like a hot-air balloon about to explode."

He let out a husky chuckle. "No worries. You can attack me anytime."

"Won't your Hinge friend mind?"

Matt ignored her question. Running a finger down her cheek, he said, "She scratched you pretty good. Be sure to wash it with antibiotic soap and put some ointment on it."

"Okay." Shelby pushed him off of her and located her panties. "Will you take me home? Mom is covering for me, and I need to get back to work."

He gave her a quizzical look. "Are you sure you're ready? You still seem shaken to me."

"I'll be fine. I have to face the music after the scene Grace and I just caused."

"You know best," Matt said, buttoning his shorts and helping Shelby to her feet.

The silence weighed heavily between them during the ride back to Magnolia Shores. As he approached the dock, Matt said, "We should talk about what just happened."

"There's nothing to discuss. I needed a friend, and you were there for me."

He cut his eyes at her, the corner of his lip curling into a smirk. "So now we're friends with benefits?"

"No, Matt. It was a one-off. It will not happen again," Shelby said, stepping off the boat and walking up the dock without looking back.

Shelby stopped by her room to clean up and change into fresh clothes. When she returned to the main house, her mom and uncle were at the receptionist's desk, attending to the mob of guests. Most were family members of the bride and groom, Sally and Bobby, who would be married at Magnolia Shores in a simple ceremony tomorrow morning at eleven.

For the next hour, Shelby handed out rum punches and helped Silas carry luggage. After the last guest had been checked in, she plopped down in a chair in front of the desk, opposite her mom and uncle. "Thank goodness you were both here. I could not have handled that alone."

Pritchard stretched his arms over his head. "That was a lesson learned for all of us. From now on, we must anticipate busy check-in days so I can be here to help you."

Kate looked over at her brother. "Don't you have a real job?"

"Actually, I turned in my notice this morning. At the end of the month, I'll be free as a bird."

"Does this mean you're going through with the expansion?" Kate asked.

"Will promised to get me numbers by the end of the week. We'll have a family meeting and make the final decision. Either way, I'm retiring. I'm tired of the travel. I can't stand to be away from Savannah and Harper, even for a day."

"Good for you. Congratulations." Kate stood up. "I'm parched. I'm going to get some bottled water. Does anyone else want one?"

In unison, Pritchard and Shelby said, "Yes, please."

Once her mother had left the room, Shelby said to her uncle, "I'm sorry about what happened earlier with Grace. It was highly unprofessional of me."

Her uncle leaned into the desk, studying her closely. "Yes, it was. But I can tell you feel bad about it, and I trust you will not let it happen again. You and Grace are very different. I can see how your personalities might clash. But she is your only sister. And family is everything. At least it is for me."

Shelby's throat swelled. "I wish things were different between Grace and me. I'm still angry she didn't ask me to be in her wedding."

"I didn't realize that. I can see how that would hurt your feelings. Try not to let it get to you." He reached across the desk for her hand. "Always strive to present your best self, regardless of how others behave. If you try to do the right thing, no matter the outcome, you'll have no regrets."

The image of Matt flashed into Shelby's mind. She harbored no regrets about their encounter. She wanted it to happen again, although she didn't hold out much hope that it would. When she mentioned the girl from Hinge, Matt had ignored her, a sign that he was likely still seeing her. She sensed the incident would be one of the defining moments of her life. For the first time, Shelby wasn't accepting the hand life dealt her—she was taking what she wanted.

ten

. . .

Grace resigned herself to sharing a room with her mother. She could endure the tiny twin bed with the extra-firm mattress for four nights. With ample room to roam about the vast acres of the property, she wouldn't have to spend a single waking hour in the stuffy cottage. On Thursday morning, she camped out at the kitchen table while her mother prepared breakfast for their guests. She used Kate's debit card to place the deposit on the band, emailed her bridesmaids the link to order their dresses, and requested catering menus from the country club. Researching bridal salons in Dallas, she identified the most exclusive high-end boutique.

"So, Mom," Grace said to Kate, who was replenishing a tray of pastries. "The first available appointment for the most prestigious bridal boutique in Dallas is on Monday, the last week of July. You've been away so long, do you think you can get off work?"

"Can't we go on the weekend?" Kate said without looking up from her task.

"They don't have any available Saturday appointments until September."

"In that case, go ahead and book the appointment. I'll figure something out with work."

"Don't sound so excited about it," Grace said in a sarcastic tone as she confirmed the appointment.

"I'm sorry, sweetheart. I have a lot on my mind." Kate took the tray into the dining room and returned with an empty fruit bowl.

Grace left the table and went to stand at the island. "Who will be in charge of breakfast when you leave on Sunday?"

"Shelby, until Izzy is fully recovered. Blossom has also offered to pitch in, but I'm not sure how long she will stay at Magnolia Shores."

Grace watched her mother spoon melon chunks from a plastic container into the bowl. Her shoulders drooped, her lips turned down, and the lines around her mouth set in a grim expression. Was she sad about leaving the Lowcountry? But why, when she had such a full life in Texas? The image of Claudia wearing her mother's robe popped into her head. Did she find out her best friend and husband were sleeping together? Was she considering leaving her dad? If she moved to South Carolina permanently, who would help Grace with the wedding?

After the breakfast shift ended, the wedding caterers took over, running Kate and Grace out of the kitchen.

"As if it isn't enough to have strangers living in your home," Grace grumbled. "Now you're allowing them to get married here too. Who in their right mind would pick Magnolia Shores for their wedding?"

"Not everyone wants a production, Grace. Some brides and grooms prefer a meaningful ceremony with only family and close friends."

"Are you saying my wedding won't be meaningful?"

Kate blushed as though realizing her gaffe. "Of course not. I guess *intimate* is a better word."

"Whatever," Grace said, leaving her mother at the back door.

From her chaise lounge at the pool, she watched florists decorate a small arbor with greenery and hot pink roses for the ceremony. At the opposite end of the terrace, catering staff members set two long tables for the luncheon that would follow.

When the ceremony began promptly at eleven, Grace moved to the hammock for a better view. The wedding gown was nothing special, a white eyelet strapless dress that grazed the floor, but the bride was gorgeous—blonde with blue eyes and a slim figure. Her radiance shone from within, clearly overjoyed to be marrying the man of her dreams. Two attendants stood with the couple—the groom's father and a bridesmaid, a younger version of the bride dressed in a pale blue sundress.

Grace felt guilty for not including her sister in the wedding party. Shelby's wholesome, girl-next-door beauty always made heads turn. Her sister was the only woman Grace knew who was prettier without makeup. Shelby's innocence was genuine, and she had no idea the impact she had on others. Grace couldn't risk having her sister steal the show on her wedding day.

When she grew bored with watching strangers pledge their eternal love for each other, Grace went for a walk on the beach. She strolled all the way to the northern tip of Sandy Island before turning back around. She spent the afternoon working on her computer at an umbrellaed table. She was dozing in a floating chair around five o'clock when she heard angry voices coming from the open balcony of the room where she'd previously been staying on the second floor.

"Who is she?" a woman screamed in a demanding voice.

"Nobody," said a man, presumably her husband. "Just a woman I met through work."

"I can't take this anymore," she shouted. "I'm leaving you."

"Yeah, right. You always say that, but you never do."

Grace caught a glimpse of the woman's brown ponytail as she slammed the balcony door shut.

"He's cheating on her. And this isn't the first time."

The voice startled Grace, and she was surprised to see Blossom floating in a chair next to her. "Where did you come from?"

"I slipped in while you were eavesdropping on that poor couple."

"I wasn't eavesdropping. I couldn't help but overhear. How do you know he's cheating on her anyway?"

Blossom let out a humph. "I know lots of things I wish I didn't."

"Makes me sad for that woman. Why doesn't she leave him?"

"Good question. Maybe she loves him? Or maybe she doesn't love herself enough. What would you do if someone you loved was being unfaithful to another person you loved? Would you tell the other person?" Blossom's emerald eyes bore into Grace, as though seeing inside her soul.

Grace squirmed. Did Blossom know about her father and Claudia? More importantly, did she know that Grace was aware of her father's affair with Claudia? "I'm not sure."

"It's not a trick question, Grace. You would have to have a darn good reason not to tell the other person."

Grace closed her eyes, shutting the woman out. When she opened her eyes again a few minutes later, Blossom had vanished, but her words remained with her the rest of the afternoon. *It's not a trick question, Grace. You would have to have a darn good reason not to tell the other person.* Grace was saving her wedding from ruin. That was a good enough reason for her to keep her father's secret.

Kate left Magnolia Shores at four-thirty for the twenty-minute drive to Beaufort. On the passenger seat beside her were the sketchbooks she'd received an hour ago from the overnight courier. Accompanying the sketchbooks was a handwritten note from Claudia expressing how much she missed Kate and valued their friendship. Kate found the note odd, given that they texted nearly every day.

Ethan Blake greeted Kate at the front door of Beaufort Abode —his partner's upscale home interior store on Bay Street. As she'd predicted, he appeared to be in his late thirties, attractive and fit with a sandy crew cut and sparkling blue eyes.

"I'm so excited to meet you! Let's go to the back where we can talk in private," he said, leading her through a maze of attractive furnishings and accessories. She smiled at the man she assumed was his partner, who was poring over fabric swatches at a worktable.

The office was handsomely appointed with leather furniture and handwoven rugs. A wall, painted a dramatic navy hue, housed a bar with a marble counter and glass shelves.

Blake opened an under-counter refrigerator. "Can I offer you a glass of wine? Champagne? Sparkling water?"

"Water is fine," she said and took the water bottle.

They sat on the sofa and chatted for a few minutes about his work as a designer.

"May I?" Ethan asked, gesturing at her sketchbooks stacked between them.

"Of course," she said, handing him the one on top. "These are my most recent designs."

Ethan flipped through the pages, making appreciative humming noises. When he finished, he skimmed through the other four books. "I'm impressed, Kate. These designs are some of the best I've seen. You have a good eye and a solid understanding of what clients want. My workshop is out back. Would you like to see my current pieces?"

"I'd love that," Kate said, already on her feet.

The wooden hut was located behind the store. A workbench took up one side of the small shop. A variety of fixtures adorned the other three walls and hung from the ceiling—pendants, copper exterior sconces, and a rectangular brass chandelier Kate fell in love with on sight. All styles were represented—traditional, contemporary, and transitional. Some pieces were edgy and others more conservative. All of them were intricately created with expertise and love.

"I don't know what to say, Ethan. These are incredible. Your craftsmanship is extraordinary. Did you design all these?"

He chuckled. "Unfortunately, my talents don't extend to the

design process. But I'm an expert at copying existing fixtures. I do it all the time for my current clients."

Kate smiled. "Which makes us the ideal partners. I design, and you produce."

Ethan leaned against his workbench. "Are you looking for a partner, Kate? Or someone to manage your production?"

"I'm not sure, honestly," Kate said, tapping her chin. She'd saved a sizable amount of money, but starting her own business terrified her. Having a partner would reduce her burden of stress. "Are you prepared to leave Beaufort Abode?"

A broad smile spread across his lips. "Heck, yes! I enjoy my job here but am ready for a change. I miss working with my hands. I've been saving for years, hoping to find the right opportunity."

Kate suddenly had more questions than answers. "I may take you up on the offer of wine. A drink would help me wrap my mind around the prospect of a partnership."

"Same. But let's go somewhere with more ambiance than my office. How does Old Bull Tavern sound?"

Kate spread her arms wide. "Anything is fine with me. Your town, your call."

They walked two blocks to the iconic tavern. When they entered, many of the local patrons called out greetings to Ethan, which spoke well to his character. They shared several appetizers and a bottle of wine. Ethan drank three glasses, but Kate limited herself to one since she was driving. They talked for more than two hours, surprised to find they agreed on most issues. Because Kate's town had more commerce, Water's Edge would be the logical location for their business. They would rent a warehouse and produce a line of pendants. Based on their success, they would develop their brand accordingly. They even agreed on the name Lumina Designs.

Ethan sat back in his chair. "I'm all in, Kate. Are you ready to move forward with developing our business plan?"

Folding her hands on the table, Kate inhaled a deep breath. "I have one small logistical problem I need to sort out. I currently live with my husband in Austin, Texas."

.

eleven

· · ·

S helby wasn't in the mood for a party. At the last minute, she informed Harper that she'd meet them at the music festival, preferring to have her own car in case she decided to leave early. For Harper's sake, since her cousin had been kind enough to include her, Shelby felt obliged to make an appearance.

Not only was Shelby still out of sorts about her argument with her sister, but her mind was consumed by thoughts of her sexual encounter with Matt on the boat. Having spent a year wallowing after her breakup with Luke, Shelby was determined not to go down that path again—dwelling on someone who wasn't into her. And she had no interest in being set up on a blind date with Cody's friend Josh What's-His-Name.

The festival venue was a large grassy field with a sandy beach fronting Catawba Sound. Harper texted her a pin, marking their location, and Shelby fought her way through the crowd. Their sizable group of friends had set up camp on the beach near the stage with picnic blankets, folding chairs, and coolers. Someone had even brought a small grill on which Harper's fiancé was cooking brats.

When he saw her, Cody set down his grilling fork and offered her a high five. "Hey, Shelby! I'm glad you made it. I want you to meet my friend Josh."

Shelby groaned inwardly. Why was Josh the first guy she met at the party?

Josh gave her a shy nod. "Nice to meet you, Shelby."

"Same," she said, barely casting a glance at him. She spotted her cousin standing at the edge of the water. "Excuse me while I go say hello to Harper."

Harper saw her coming and threw her arms wide. "Yay! You're here." She lowered her voice. "I saw you talking to Josh. Isn't he adorable?"

"I guess," Shelby said, fighting back tears. "I'm sorry, Harper. I'm in a rotten mood. I probably shouldn't have come."

Harper dropped her smile. "Oh, no! What's wrong? Is it Matt?"

Shelby bit down on her quivering lip. "That, and I got in a bad fight with my sister yesterday."

"Aww, sweetie. That's too bad." Harper pulled Shelby in for a half hug. "Forget about Josh. I want you to meet some of my girlfriends. Can you at least stay for a little while?"

"Sure. Why not?" Shelby said in a strained tone of enthusiasm.

Harper called her friends over, and they gathered around Shelby, introducing themselves and asking her where she was from. One young woman caught Shelby's attention. Callie had a bohemian charm, with her dark chocolate hair cascading in layers around her face. She wore a pink tunic, cutoff jean shorts, and cowboy boots. The yellow flecks in her warm brown eyes sparkled with excitement as she discussed the lineup of bands scheduled to perform over the weekend.

When the first band appeared on stage, Callie took Shelby by the hand. "Come on. This band is the best if you like classic rock."

Callie dragged Shelby to the front of the crowd at the edge of the stage, where they danced for over an hour. When they returned to the others, Shelby admitted to Harper, "I have a girl crush on Callie."

Harper grinned, her eyes on Callie. "Isn't she the best? She's Josh's twin sister."

Shelby's jaw dropped. "What? Are you serious?"

"Yep. And he's every bit as awesome." Harper nudged Shelby. "Where's the harm in talking to him?"

"Maybe I will." As she scanned the crowd for Josh, Shelby's eyes landed on Matt who was hugging a young woman with golden hair from behind as they swayed to the music.

Harper followed Shelby's gaze. "I was hoping you wouldn't see him. She's the girl he was with at the Clam and Claw. The one he met on Hinge."

Shelby's stomach knotted as she watched Matt pull her closer and bury his face in her neck. She thought about all the times he'd kissed Shelby, his soft lips and the feel of his muscular body pressed against hers.

Let it go, Shelby, she told herself. *He doesn't want you.*

As she turned her back on Matt, Shelby found herself face-to-face with Josh. "Oh. Hi."

"Hey there. I saw you dancing with my sister. I figured you might be thirsty." He handed her a bottle of water. "If you'd rather have a beer, there's plenty in the cooler."

"I'm fine with water." Shelby smiled at him, studying his face. He had dark hair like his sister, but his eyes were deep blue like the ocean. Harper was right. He was adorable. "The resemblance is uncanny. Are you as much fun as Callie?"

His smile curved into dimples. "Depends on your idea of fun. Callie thrives on large parties like these." He swept an arm at the crowd. "I prefer smaller, more intimate gatherings."

Something about the way he said *intimate* sent butterflies buzzing around in Shelby's belly. "Do you and Callie get along?"

He nodded. "We do, despite our different personalities. We are currently working together to expand our family's landscape business. Callie is establishing herself as a landscape designer, and I've started a lawn care service catering to high-end clients."

Shelby ignored the pang of envy. She and Grace would never get along, let alone go into business together. But she was grateful for her blossoming relationship with her new cousin. Hopefully, she and Harper would soon be working together to decorate The Sanctuary.

Josh gestured at the banquet table. "Are you hungry? There's a ton of food over there."

"Sure! Food sounds good," she said, having worked up an appetite on the dance floor.

They filled their plates and helped themselves to soft drinks from the cooler. Josh easily navigated the social scene, introducing Shelby to his friends as Harper's cousin. They were all older than her, predominantly in their upper twenties and early thirties. Still, Shelby had no problem conversing about careers, weddings, and the arrival of their first babies.

"How old are you, Josh?" she asked when they found themselves standing alone.

"Twenty-eight. And you?"

"I'll be twenty-five in August. Do you think that's too young?"

His dark brows became one. "Not at all. Why?"

"Just checking," she said with a smile and excused herself to go to the restroom.

She was waiting in line for her turn at the porta potties when a familiar voice behind her said, "Are you having fun?"

A shiver traveled her spine. "I'm having a blast. Thanks for asking," she said without turning to face him.

He spun her around. "You look amazing," he said in a throaty voice, yellow flecks in his eyes aglow.

"Save the compliment for your date. Coincidentally, she might consider toning down her hair color. It's too yellow to be natural," Shelby said, although she secretly suspected his date was a true blonde.

"Ouch. Why are you so hostile? I hope you're not mad at me for what happened in the boat. Because you're the one who attacked me," Matt said, placing a hand on Shelby's hip and pulling her close.

Smacking his hand away, she jumped back as though she'd been burned. "I was having a moment that day. I was furious at my sister, and you happened to be there. Obviously, it didn't mean anything to either of us, so let's forget it happened."

"Consider it forgotten. Are you dating Josh Morgan now?" Matt asked with a smug smile.

"We just met, but he seems like a nice guy, and he doesn't care that I'm only twenty-four. Goodbye, Matt," Shelby said and moved to the front of the line.

When she emerged from the porta potty, Matt was nowhere in sight. Instead of returning to the group, Shelby located her car and left the festival.

She was halfway home when Harper texted.

Are you okay? Why'd you disappear?

Shelby waited until she was stopped at a red light to respond.

Sorry. We have a full house this weekend and I need to check on our guests.

Bummer. Josh will be disappointed. Can I give him your number?

The light turned green, and she continued across the Merriweather Bridge. Her brief *thing* with Matt had been more of a flirtation than a fling. Yet she was still reeling from it, and she couldn't stop thinking about him. Maybe she needed a distraction, something to occupy her time and make her feel less empty inside. Besides, Josh seemed like a good guy. Perhaps he wouldn't hurt her like all the others.

When she arrived home, Shelby parked the car and turned off the engine. Magnolia Shores was like the end of the earth. She could easily live here like a hermit, but she wasn't ready to give up on her social life just yet.

She thumbed off the text to her cousin.

Sure.

twelve

. . .

After a sleepless night, Kate slipped out of bed and tiptoed around the room as she dressed, careful not to wake her sleeping daughter. She left the cottage and crossed the courtyard. The sky was growing lighter with the approaching dawn as she cut through the sand dunes to the beach.

On her stroll north, she talked to God as she often did during quiet moments. She was at a crossroads, and she needed guidance. Ethan had been disappointed when she told him about her life in Texas, but she assured him she'd figure something out, even if it meant splitting time between Austin and Water's Edge.

Kate's marriage had been steadily declining for years. She hadn't missed Rand these past few weeks any more than he had missed her. Rand and Izzy had never been close—like many mothers-in-law and sons-in-law, they tolerated each other for the sake of their daughter/wife. But Rand had shown deep concern for Izzy's health immediately after her stroke. However, that concern vanished once she came out of the coma, and he hadn't returned Kate's calls since. His only texts were about house-related matters.

> When do the trashmen come? Should I schedule an irrigation checkup?

Kate experienced an epiphany as the first pink rays of sun peeked over the horizon. Izzy stood in the way of Kate getting her inheritance. Once her mother died, the family's vast fortune would pass to Kate and Pritchard. Although Rand enjoyed a prosperous career as a cardiac surgeon, he came from a humble background, and the wealth Kate stood to inherit would dramatically alter their lives. Was it possible Rand was only staying with Kate for her money? There was only one way to find out.

She tugged her phone out of her pocket and typed out a text to her husband.

> Izzy has suffered another stroke. It doesn't look good.

As she pressed Send, she squeezed her eyes shut and apologized to God for lying.

When she looked up again, Blossom stood before her, shaking her head and clucking her tongue. "That was naughty, Kate. Shame on you."

"Naughty but necessary." Kate flashed her phone at Blossom. "If my husband is only after my money, I can't stay with him."

Jolene whined in response to Kate's hostile tone. Blossom picked Jolene up and tucked her under her arm. "I understand you need the truth, but what you did was deceitful. What if he calls your daughters? How will you explain your lie?"

"You're right. I wouldn't want to alarm them. But I can't retract the text. I'll think of something to tell the girls."

"Good luck with that." Blossom set her squirming dog down, and Jolene took off chasing a flock of seagulls. "I've been wondering about my next mission. Now that I've been assigned to your case, I can stay at this tropical oasis longer."

Kate frowned. "What're you talking about? What case?"

"A few minutes ago, when you were talking to God, you asked for guidance," Blossom said, tilting her face heavenward. "My elders heard you, and since I'm already here, I'm the logical one to provide it."

Kate gripped Blossom's arm. "Excellent! I need a guardian angel to face what's coming my way. I'm glad I sent the text to Rand. Austin is an hour behind us. If he responds as I suspect, he'll call as soon as he wakes up, which should be around eight o'clock our time. What should I tell him?"

Blossom pried Kate's fingers off her arm. "Oh no, you don't. I'll lose my wings if you drag me into your deceitful ploy. I can offer advice, but I will not conspire."

"I stand corrected." She kissed Blossom's cheek. "If you don't mind, I need a few minutes alone to think."

Blossom nodded. "Take your time, love bug. I'll head back to the kitchen and get started on breakfast."

Kate watched Jolene and Blossom saunter off before continuing north toward the Sandy Island Club. Blossom was right. Her impulsive plan was deceitful. But her husband's response would be very telling.

Kate turned toward home. She couldn't tell her girls that she'd lied to their father. She would have to take her chances and hope he didn't contact them. But just in case, she would do damage control.

When she knocked on Shelby's door, her daughter answered with a muffled, "Who is it?"

"It's me, sweetheart. Mom."

A sleepy Shelby came to the door in her pajamas with mussed hair and mascara-smeared cheeks. "What're you doing here? Is something wrong?"

"I was on my way to the kitchen, and I wanted to see your room. Since I'll be leaving soon, I'd like to be able to picture you in your space."

Shelby rubbed her eyes. "Aww. That's sweet. Come on in. I need to get up anyway."

Kate followed Shelby into the room and sat on the edge of the twin bed. "I can't believe I've never been in this room. It's cozy."

"Cozy is an understatement. There's barely enough room to turn around in here. But I don't mind. At least I don't have to share with Grace. You look sad. Are you sure there's nothing wrong?" Shelby asked, slipping on a sweatshirt over her camisole.

Kate inhaled a deep breath. "I'm positive. Have you heard from your father?"

Shelby picked up her phone from the nightstand and thumbed through her messages. "Nope. The last I heard from him was while Izzy was still in a coma." She narrowed her teal eyes at Kate. "Are you two fighting again?"

Kate pursed her lips. "What makes you ask that?"

"Because all you ever do is fight." Shelby fastened her messy hair back in an elastic band and sat beside Kate on the bed. "I feel sorry for you, Mama. You deserve to be happy. I don't blame you if you divorce him. He's changed. He's not the same dad from when I was young."

Kate picked at a loose thread on the bedspread. "Oh? How so?"

"He used to take us on fun outings, bring pizza home from Antonio's all the time, and give us meaningful Christmas gifts. He hasn't done any of that in years."

Shelby was right. Rand hadn't been himself for a long time. Maybe he was going through a midlife crisis. "I thought I was the only one who'd noticed."

"You've seemed so much happier since you've been in South Carolina. Why don't you move here permanently?"

Shelby made it sound so simple. Could she really move to the Lowcountry for good? "Who knows? Maybe one day I will." Kate stood to go. "I'm so proud of you, sweetheart. You've become a remarkable young woman."

Shelby smiled. "Because of you. Not only did you raise me right, you had the courage to kick me out of the house."

"I didn't kick you out of the house, Shelby. I bought you an airline ticket and arranged for your job."

Shelby giggled. "At the time, I felt like I was being kicked out. But Magnolia Shores is the best thing that's ever happened to me. I'm finally figuring out who I really am."

Kate kissed Shelby's cheek. "I can see that. It's a good look for you."

"The Lowcountry is a good look for you too, Mama."

Kate left the pool house and went straight to the cottage, shaking her eldest awake from a deep sleep.

Grace sat up straight in bed. "Mom! What's wrong? What time is it?" She glanced at the clock on the nightstand. "Ugh. It's not even eight o'clock. What're you doing here so early? You're divorcing Dad, aren't you?"

Kate reared her head back as though she'd been slapped. "What? No."

Grace kicked off the covers and threw her legs over the side of the bed, her bare feet landing on the wood floor with a loud thud. "If you divorce him, you'll ruin my wedding."

Kate's mind reeled. What had gotten into her daughter? "Our marriage has nothing to do with your wedding, Grace."

"The hell it doesn't. You'll end up hating each other, and your hostility will make everyone uncomfortable at the wedding. And what if Dad decides he won't pay for the reception?"

Grace was borderline hysterical. Whatever had set her off, Kate needed to calm her down. "That won't happen, sweetheart. Your father has been saving for your wedding for years."

"Mom, please! Can't you wait until after the wedding to divorce him?"

Kate blinked hard, not believing her ears. "Would you listen to yourself? Are you really this self-centered?"

"I'm sorry, Mom. But this is my big day. I need you front and center. I don't want you all distracted and mopey."

Kate's anger surged. She would say something she regretted if she didn't leave the room. "We'll talk later when you've cooled off," she said, hurrying out of the cottage.

Kate strode angrily to the garden and paced around the fountain as she replayed the scene in her mind. Why was Grace so convinced they were getting a divorce? Did she know something Kate didn't know? She was taking deep breaths, trying to clear her head before going to the kitchen, when she received a call from her boss.

"Morning, Diane," Kate said in a feigned chipper voice. "You're at work early."

"I'm afraid I'm calling with bad news, Kate. You've been demoted. Bonnie is taking your place, effective immediately."

"What? Why? I don't understand."

Diane let out a loud sigh. "This wasn't my decision. It came from the top. Management is impressed with the job Bonnie has been doing in your absence, and they believe she deserves a promotion."

"In other words, they can pay her half what they're paying me, never mind my twenty-five years of loyalty to the company." Kate remembered that Diane said demoted, not fired. "What's my new job title?"

"Sales associate," Diane said in a barely audible voice.

Kate's heart sank. All her hard work had been erased in the blink of an eye. "Why not just fire me?"

"Honestly? They want to avoid paying you a severance package."

Kate gripped the phone as her anger skyrocketed. "Let me get this straight. I took my first personal leave in twenty-five years to be with my mother after she suffered a debilitating stroke, and you promised me multiple times that my job was secure. I'm pretty sure I have grounds for a lawsuit. I quit, Diane. Tell management I'll see them in court."

Stuffing her phone in her pocket, Kate followed the gravel path to the kitchen. She filled a glass with water from the sink and gulped it down.

"What's wrong, Katie girl? Did you hear from your husband?" Blossom asked from the stove where she was browning chicken sausage patties in a skillet.

Kate drank a second glass of water and collapsed against the counter. "No! I heard from my boss. I just got demoted at work," she said, watching closely for Blossom's reaction.

The woman didn't flinch. "What did they say when you quit?"

Kate's hair stood on end. "How did you know I quit? Did you arrange for my demotion, Blossom?"

Blossom let out a belly laugh. "Nah. That was coming. I just helped it along. You need to be free to make the important choices that lie ahead."

"What choices? What if I wanted to keep my job?"

Blossom set down her spatula and shortened the distance between them. "If that's the case, you've been sending me the wrong signals. My strong intuition tells me you want to stay in the Lowcountry permanently."

Kate dropped her gaze, her tears blurring the worn braided rug. "I do, Blossom. More than I've ever wanted anything in my life. I just have no idea how to make that happen."

Blossom engulfed her in a hug. "That's why I'm here. But brace yourself, love bug. The ride is about to get turbulent."

thirteen

· · ·

Her mother's words echoed in Grace's mind as she took her coffee to the beach. *Would you listen to yourself? Are you really this self-centered?* Grace admitted she'd been *acting* self-centered lately. Her wedding was at stake, the most important day of her life. But she wasn't *actually* self-centered. Or was she? Wyatt had called her a Bridezilla. Was that the same thing?

Lost in her own thoughts, Grace paid little attention to the woman setting up her beach chair nearby until the woman's soft crying snapped her back to reality. Shifting in her chair for a better look, Grace realized she was the woman from the balcony whose husband was cheating on her. Couldn't she cry somewhere else? She was interrupting Grace's peace and quiet.

When the crying grew louder, Grace moved her chair farther down the beach. She scrolled through social media on her phone and responded to a few work emails, but her thoughts kept drifting back to her mother. She admitted she'd overreacted earlier. But Kate had woken Grace from a disturbing dream about her wedding. Her father was parading down the aisle with Grace on one arm and Claudia on the other. Seated in the front pew was her mother, who was bawling loud enough for the entire congregation to hear.

A horrifying thought struck Grace, and she thumbed through her phone for Claudia's text. *I haven't told Rand about our run-in this morning. For everyone's sake, I suggest we keep this between us.*

What if Claudia tried to break up with her father? He would naturally want to know why. If Claudia confessed to seeing Grace in the kitchen on Monday, he would fly to South Carolina to patch things up with her mom. Kate would be furious when she found out Grace knew about his affair. Then Shelby would get involved because she was always sticking her nose where it didn't belong. A family feud would ensue, and they'd have to call off her wedding.

Panic set in, and Grace's chest tightened, making it difficult to breathe. Her skin crawled, sweat trickled down her back, and she felt bugs in her hair. When she could take it no more, she folded her chair and went up to the pool.

The newlyweds and their younger family members were playing Marco Polo in the pool while the older folks watched from lounge chairs. Locating a vacant chair, Grace stretched out and searched for wedding gowns on her phone.

When the crying woman with the cheating husband came up from the beach, the woman sitting next to Grace frantically waved her over. "Yoo-hoo, Susan! There's an empty chair over here."

So the woman with the cheating husband's name is Susan, Grace thought. *Crying Susan.*

Grace considered her escape options. The cottage was out of the question. She wasn't in the mood to make nice to Izzy and her caregiver. After her irrational behavior earlier, she wasn't yet ready to face her mother. The beach no longer appealed to her. She sank down in her chair, closing her eyes and willing those people to go away.

Crying Susan and her friend talked so loudly that Grace couldn't tune them out. From their conversation, she learned that Susan was the bride's first cousin, and the other woman, Jennifer, was married to Susan's brother. When Jennifer asked Susan why she didn't seem like herself, Susan started crying again. She blubbered on about her husband's affair, telling Jennifer way more than Grace ever wanted to know about Susan's love life.

Grace stuffed her earpods in and selected a playlist from her Spotify app. She finally dozed off, and when she opened her eyes again, Blossom was staring at her, inches from her face.

"Blossom! What're you doing?" Grace asked, crawling up the back of the chair to get away from her.

Blossom laughed. "Don't worry, sunshine. I was just checking on you, making sure you were still breathing," she said, plopping down on the lounge chair beside her.

Grace glanced around, shaking off the cobwebs of sleep as she tried to get her bearings. The wedding party had left the pool and moved to the tables, where they were enjoying a picnic lunch. Blossom's little dog was standing on the pool's edge, staring into the water.

"Your gramma doesn't allow dogs in the pool," Blossom explained.

Grace peered at Blossom over the top of her sunglasses. "Since when? My grandfather's yellow lab used to swim in the pool all the time."

"Beats me. I usually wait until she goes to physical therapy to let her swim."

"Shame on you, Blossom. You don't strike me as a rule breaker."

"Depends on the rule," Blossom said, tossing a bouncy rubber ball into the pool. Jolene jumped into the pool after it and paddled around. "Look at her smile. Why would you deprive a dog of such happiness?"

Grace chuckled as she watched the dog. "I agree wholeheartedly. *No dogs in the pool* is a rule worth breaking."

Jolene retrieved the ball and swam to the steps. Instead of returning the ball to Blossom, she dropped it on the pool deck and trotted over to the tables, sniffing for scraps of food at the feet of the wedding family.

Crying Susan was seated at one of the tables with a man Grace assumed was her husband. She batted her eyelashes and flashed him a broad smile.

"I guess they made up," Grace mumbled.

Blossom followed her gaze. "Mm-hmm. Looks like it."

"Why would she stay with him when he continues to be unfaithful to her?"

"Love, fear, money—whatever the reason, she's making her own choices. Your mama deserves to know the truth so she can make the right choice for herself."

Grace swiveled her head toward her. "I don't understand. How could you possibly know about my dad's affair?"

"I have my ways. Your mama has some big life-changing decisions to make, sunshine. Learning her husband has been sleeping with her best friend is an important factor in making those decisions. She quit her job this morning. Her marriage is now the only thing standing in the way of her moving home to her beloved Magnolia Shores."

"But they can't get divorced. They love each other."

"Do you know that for sure? It's common for men and women to fall out of love after decades of marriage."

Grace folded her arms over her chest. "Then they should go for couple's therapy. They have to try to make it work for the sake of . . ." Her voice trailed off.

"The sake of what, Grace? Your wedding? A wedding is a meaningful ceremony between a man and a woman with God as their witness. All the hoopla—the reception, the wedding party, the honeymoon—is the proverbial icing on the cake. Is the hoopla worth sacrificing your mama's happiness?"

"Mind your own business, Blossom. You don't know what you're talking about." Tears filled Grace's eyes, and she looked away. When she glanced back a minute later, Blossom was floating around in the pool with Jolene.

Grace pulled her sunhat low and slid down in her lounge chair. She had never considered whether her mother was happy. Truth be told, she didn't think of Kate as a woman. She was her mom, whose primary purpose on earth was to raise Grace, which included planning her wedding. Was this the change Grace had noticed in her mother? Did Kate prefer living at Magnolia Shores with Izzy, her brother, and her youngest daughter? Without the presence of the husband she no longer loved or her Bridezilla oldest daughter.

Grace shrugged off her concern. Blossom was a virtual stranger. She didn't understand their family. Grace had dreamed of this fairy-tale wedding all her life. Her parents' situation would work itself out without Grace's interference.

fourteen

· · ·

Kate was studying her most recent lighting designs at the kitchen table when she heard angry voices and the crashing sound of something breaking in a room overhead. Getting up from the table, she hurried up the stairs. Another member of the wedding family greeted her in the hallway.

"I'm sorry. They're having some problems," said the family member. "I'll ask them to keep it down."

Kate gave her a curt nod. "Please do. Or I'll have to call security."

When she returned to the kitchen, Kate found Pritchard thumbing through her sketchbook. He looked up when she entered the room. "These are excellent, Kate. Are you planning to produce them?"

"I hope so." Kate held up her hands to show fingers crossed. "I've found a craftsman who is interested in forming a partnership. He's very talented, a true artisan."

"Good for you," Pritchard said, closing the sketchbook. "Will you establish this partnership in the Lowcountry?"

"That's the idea. Ethan lives in Beaufort. We are thinking of renting industrial space here in Water's Edge. But I have a few things to figure out about my personal life before I commit."

"If you're talking about your husband, I'm in favor of you leaving him."

Kate planted a hand on her hip. "When did you develop such animosity toward my husband?"

"Since I first met him."

Kate studied his face, unable to read his expression. "You're lying."

Pritchard pressed his lips into a grim smile. "Unfortunately, I'm not. I tolerated Rand because you were in love with him. But I've never approved of the way he treats you."

"He's a cardiac surgeon, Pritch. He saves lives. So what if my needs come second to his patients."

"It's more than that, Kate. He condescends to you. He acts like he's better than you."

Kate wasn't in the mood for an argument she couldn't win. Changing the subject, she asked, "What're you up to today?"

Pritchard waved a cardboard tube. "I'm going to show Izzy the plans for The Sanctuary. I got numbers from Will and—"

The sound of the front door slamming echoed down the hall, and Shelby burst into the room. "Pritchard! I saw your car out front! Did you get Will's proposal?"

"I was just talking to your mom about that." Pritchard set the tube on the table and went to the refrigerator, pouring himself a glass of sweet tea. He held the pitcher up. "Does anyone else want some?"

Shelby and Kate both shook their heads.

He guzzled down the tea and poured himself another glass.

Kate and Shelby exchanged looks of exasperation. "Out with it, Pritchard," Kate said, and Shelby added, "The suspense is killing us."

"The numbers are way more than I expected. Inflation has driven up the cost of building materials, and labor costs are at an all-time high. We have the money to expand, but a large chunk of our inheritance would be invested in the building if the resort flops. Then what would we do?"

"The land alone is worth a small fortune," Kate said. "We would sell Magnolia Shores and buy Mom a small beach cottage."

"But Magnolia Shores has been in our family for generations," Pritchard argued.

"I realize that, Pritch. But Dad understood the risks when he laid out his plans."

Shelby raised her hand to speak. "The resort won't fail unless something drastic happens. We're fully booked until Labor Day, and guests are already inquiring about next summer. Magnolia Shores is a special place. Once The Sanctuary is complete and we've added all the extra amenities, word will spread about our spectacular destination."

Kate nodded her agreement. "The new building will make us one of the hottest up-and-coming resorts on the East Coast."

Pritchard's shoulders sagged with the burden of his decision.

Kate gave his shoulder a squeeze. "Let's take the onus off of you and let Mom decide."

"Great idea. Let's do it." Dumping his ice in the sink, Pritchard grabbed the cardboard tube containing the blueprints and exited the back door.

As they followed Pritchard across the courtyard, Shelby told Kate, "I have a date tonight. Would you be able to cover for me at the front desk?"

"Of course, sweetheart. Who's the lucky guy?"

"A friend of Harper and Cody's. I met him at the music festival."

"Is he taking you out to dinner?"

Shelby smiled. "I'm not sure. He was somewhat mysterious about his plan. He's picking me up at seven, so I assume we'll eat something at some point. He told me to dress casually."

"Well, I hope you have fun. Have you heard from your father?" Rand had yet to respond to Kate's text, and she was increasingly anxious about his continued silence.

Shelby shook her head. "Nope. Why do you keep asking me that?"

"No reason. I haven't heard from him lately, and I'm worried about him."

"Dad's a big boy. He can take care of himself."

Izzy was reading a novel when the threesome filed into the cottage. "Something's wrong. What happened?" she asked, her face etched with concern.

"Nothing, Mother. Everything is fine. We want to show you the plans for The Sanctuary."

"Okay." Izzy closed her paperback and patted the sofa beside her. "Sit down."

Pritchard and Kate sandwiched their mother on the sofa, each holding one end of the blueprints, and Shelby sat in front of them on the edge of the coffee table. Pritchard used an ink pen to point out the public rooms on the main floor.

Izzy's breath hitched, and her hand flew to her mouth when he showed her the full-color elevation plans. "It's very Lowcountry, so befitting the property. What do you all think?"

Kate looked to Pritchard to answer for them. "We love it. We want your blessing to move forward with construction."

"Do I get to move back into my house?" Izzy asked.

"Of course, as long as you understand we'll occasionally need to use some of the rooms for overflow."

Izzy considered this. "I guess that would be all right."

Shelby squeezed her grandmother's hand. "Not only that, we're counting on you to help us run the resort. As we discussed, you'll have important duties as wildlife expert, historian, and hostess of afternoon tea."

Izzy beamed. "Then count me in. You have my blessing. Shelby, get me my cane." She gestured at her cane, which was looped over the arm of a nearby chair. "This calls for a celebration. Let's go over to the kitchen, and you can mix us up one of your concoctions."

Shelby leaped to her feet. "Cool! We'll name the drink The Sanctuary. I've been wanting to experiment with a cucumber cilantro margarita. Hopefully, we have the necessary ingredients."

"If not, my caregiver is at the market, picking up a few items for the cottage. She can grab whatever we need."

Although they moved at a snail's pace to the main house, Kate was thrilled her mother had graduated from a walker to a cane.

Pritchard pulled Kate aside while Shelby and Izzy studied the refrigerator's contents. "Do you mind if I look at your designs again? I have an idea."

"Of course not," Kate said, sitting down at the table with him. "I have four more sketchbooks in the cottage if you'd like to see those."

"Do they have nautical elements like these?"

"Some do. But these are the best."

Pritchard expressed sounds of satisfaction—oohs and ahhs—as he turned the pages. Finally, he sat back in his chair. "How would you feel about me hiring you to provide the fixtures for The Sanctuary?"

Kate blinked wide, her jaw hitting the table. "Are you serious? With the right marketing, this could put Lumina Designs on the map."

"That's the idea. What do you think of making some of the more prominent fixtures exclusive to The Sanctuary?"

"Yes! I love that idea. We'll give them Lowcountry-sounding names relevant to Magnolia Shores." Kate hesitated. "Do you really think they're good enough, Pritchard?" she asked, her tone of voice more serious.

"You're a lighting expert. You know they are. But since you're just starting out, we would have to agree on a production schedule."

Kate massaged her chin. "Of course. I would need to consult with Ethan. I'm not sure how fast he works. If nothing else, we could produce the fixtures for the public rooms."

"Talk to him and let me know. Does this mean you're staying in the Lowcountry?" her brother asked with a boyish grin.

"Worst case scenario, I'll travel back and forth." The idea

didn't excite Kate nearly as much as the prospect of moving to the Lowcountry. But she had her marriage to consider.

Izzy's caregiver arrived with the ingredients for Shelby's concoction, and they all gathered around the island while she worked.

Shelby was pouring the first sips for everyone when Grace entered through the back door. "What's with all the commotion? I heard you all outside."

"We're celebrating!" said a giddy Izzy.

Grace approached the counter. "Cool! What're we celebrating?"

"Life!" Kate said with a little too much enthusiasm. When Izzy looked at her across the counter, Kate shook her head slightly, signaling not to say more about The Sanctuary.

"We're celebrating my new drink, a cucumber cilantro margarita." Shelby poured a splash of green liquid into a salt-rimmed glass and handed it to her sister. "Here. Try some."

Grace took a tentative sip, smacked her lips, and scrunched up her face. "Too tart for me. You should rethink your mixology career." She set the glass down. "I'm going for a walk on the beach," she said, disappearing out the back door.

"Why didn't you tell her the truth?" Izzy asked, her brow pinched.

"Grace loves social media, and I figured you'd want to keep The Sanctuary a secret until you make a formal announcement. That's a public relations opportunity you don't want to miss." Truthfully, Kate didn't want Grace to tell her father they were investing a considerable chunk of her inheritance to expand the resort.

"That's a brilliant idea, Kate! We need to hire a marketing person right away." Pritchard held up his glass. "To The Sanctuary!"

As everyone clinked glasses, Kate slipped outside to call Ethan. When he answered, she explained about The Sanctuary and Pritchard's offer of an exclusive lighting deal.

"I'm floored, Kate. We'll figure out a way to meet his production schedule. Once we've nailed the prototypes, we'll hire additional artisans. We must get to work right away. We need to hire an attorney to write our partnership agreement. Are you free early next week to start looking for warehouse space?"

"Actually, I'm leaving for Austin on Sunday. I'm not sure when I'll be back. I need a little time to figure out my personal life."

"I sense some hesitancy on your part, Kate," Ethan said, his tone now tinged with irritation. "With all due respect, I can't risk my life savings on a business partnership with someone who isn't fully committed."

After ending the call, Kate dropped down to a nearby bench. She didn't blame Ethan for being upset. She was acting like a flake, making plans for a new life when her current one was unsettled. She couldn't let this opportunity slip away, but she couldn't string Ethan along either. She wanted this so badly she could taste it, yet something was holding her back.

fifteen

. . .

J osh texted at six o'clock.

> Change of plans. Wear your bathing suit. Can I
> pick you up early at six thirty?

She promptly responded.

> Sure! I'll be ready.

Hurrying to her room, she changed into a bathing suit and cover-up and was waiting on the front stoop when he texted again.

> Meet me on the dock.

Shelby frowned. The dock? He must be picking her up in a boat.

She thumbed off a text as she crossed the courtyard to the dock.

> Coming.

Josh's center console fishing boat was approximately the same size as Matt's, although a nicer and newer version. Giving her a hand on board, he took her tote bag from her and stowed it in a covered cubby at the bow. She sat beside him in the comfortable leather captain's chairs, an upgrade from Matt's leaning post.

"Where are we going?" she asked.

"It's a surprise," he said, navigating the boat away from the dock. "We have a short ride to our destination. Would you prefer the ocean or sound?"

"The ocean if it's calm enough."

"Excellent choice. I already checked. The ocean is calm as glass," he said, pushing the throttles forward.

As they rounded the tip of Sandy Island, she checked him out from the corner of her eye. His dark hair was windblown, and he wore tortoise Wayfarer sunglasses, a pink polo shirt, and khaki board shorts. He smelled deliciously clean, like a cool breeze on an early summer morning. At the music festival, she'd been too distracted by the crowd and Matt to notice his striking features and muscular body.

When they reached the ocean, he slowed his speed as they moved up the coast. He retrieved his phone from the console. "What's your preference—reggae, alt-rock, or country?"

"Hmm, let's see. It feels like a reggae kind of night to me."

"I agree." He selected the playlist, and Ziggy Marley spilled from a hidden speaker.

"Where do you keep your boat?" Shelby asked.

"At my parents' house. They live on the town side of the sound."

"Is it near Marsh Point?"

"Marsh Point is on Pelican's Way. We're on Cypress Court, the next street closer to town. I'll show you on the way home. Do you know the Darbys?"

"Yes! Savannah is my aunt. She grew up at Marsh Point, but her sister now owns the house."

Josh nodded. "Right. I take care of Ashton's lawn. Callie and I recently collaborated on a large installation for her brother, Will, across the street."

"That's cool. Do you live with your parents?"

"No. I rent a carriage house in town from a nice lady, Muriel Richardson. She gives me a good rent rate in exchange for—"

Shelby cut him off. "Taking care of her yard?"

Josh smiled. "And her pool and her dog when she's out of town. She often visits her children, who are scattered all over the country."

"Sounds like a sweet deal."

"It is. The carriage house is seriously cool."

"Look, dolphins!" Shelby said, pointing at the school of dolphins off the starboard side.

His eyes followed her finger. "Aren't they incredible? I love watching them."

When they approached the northern tip of the island, Josh pulled up to the dock of the contemporary house that had been built within the past couple of years.

"What're you doing?" Shelby asked, confused. "Do you know the people who live here?"

"I work for them," he said with a mischievous grin.

"Let me guess. You take care of their yard, pool, and house when they're out of town."

"Pretty much. The Mathesons live full-time in Connecticut. This is their vacation home. They were here last week for the Fourth of July, and they'll be back for the month of August," Josh said, fastening a line to the cleat.

"They don't mind us being here?" Shelby asked, retrieving her tote bag from the compartment where he had stored it.

"Not at all. Mr. Matheson pays me to spend time here. My presence wards off any nefarious people stalking the house." Josh grabbed a soft Yeti cooler from the stern. "I packed us a picnic."

Shelby's eyes widened. "A picnic? I'm impressed."

"Don't be. It's nothing fancy."

They walked side by side up the dock. When they reached the

pool, Josh spread the contents of his cooler on a small teak table—warmed chicken tenders, veggies with sour cream dip, and egg salad sandwich quarters. Shelby loved that he'd taken the time and care to prepare such a thoughtful picnic.

"I hope you like rosé," he said, opening a bottle of wine.

"I love rosé," Shelby said.

He poured the pink wine into two stemless plastic cups, and they sat on the edge of the infinity pool with their feet in the water and a bag of pistachios between them. The sun had begun its descent, casting an orange glow over the sound.

"Is the view this spectacular at Magnolia Shores?" Josh asked.

"Pretty much." Her eyes traveled the perimeter of the property. "Although I think the elevation is higher here. You'll have to come over sometime. We can grill out, and you can judge for yourself."

He popped a handful of nuts in his mouth. "I'd like that. Are you here for the summer? Or are you planning to live in Water's Edge full-time?"

"If you had asked me a month ago, I would've given you a different answer. But I've fallen in love with this place, and I hope I never have to leave. I'm fortunate to have a rare career opportunity at Magnolia Shores."

"What exactly is your job at the bed and breakfast?" Josh asked.

"My title is reservations manager, but my uncle and I run the B&B together. I'm not supposed to talk about it, so don't say anything, but we plan to expand."

His blue eyes sparkled. "Seriously? That's cool. Can you tell me anything else about this expansion?"

Shelby hesitated. While she felt she could trust him, she would hate for news of their expansion to leak out. "I wish I could, but I promised I wouldn't. I'll be able to tell you more soon."

"I understand." He tugged his shirt over his head and slid off the side of the pool into the water. "Get in. The water is a perfect eighty-two degrees."

Shelby took off her cover-up and joined him in the water. They treaded water, splashed around, and floated on noodles, discussing their common interests. He was easy to talk to, and she genuinely enjoyed his company. When he kissed her at the end of the night, instead of the burning passion she had felt with Matt, she experienced a comforting sense of tranquility washing over her.

Grace's call to Wyatt rang once before going to voicemail. He hadn't responded to her calls or texts all week, but declining her call was confirmation that her fiancé was avoiding her. She left a short message. "Wyatt, please call me back. I'm worried about you."

She sipped her chamomile tea while staring at her phone, willing it to ring. Ten minutes passed before he called. She picked up right away, answering with a perky, "Hey, babe! Is everything okay?"

"Everything's fine," he said in a tone that suggested otherwise.

Nerves clinched her gut, and she started babbling, "I'm so glad you suggested I come to South Carolina to see Mom. We've accomplished a lot on the wedding planning front. We've made the deposit on the band. The bridesmaids have ordered their dresses—"

"Grace! Stop! I don't want to hear about the wedding."

The earth fell out from beneath Grace. "So something *is* wrong. What is it, Wyatt?"

"I moved back in with my parents."

"Wait! What? Why?" She swung her legs over the lounge chair and began pacing beside the pool, chewing a fingernail. She hadn't taken him seriously when he threatened to move in with his parents.

"Either you've changed, or this wedding is bringing out the

worst in you. You've become a total diva, and I can't take it anymore. I don't want a big wedding. I told you that."

Grace stopped pacing. "When? I don't remember you ever saying that."

"Right after we got engaged. I said it several times, but you completely ignored me."

Grace racked her brain. She didn't remember him ever expressing interest in having a small wedding. "So you're breaking up with me because I want a big wedding?"

"I never said I was breaking up with you. That's part of the problem, Grace. You don't listen to me anymore."

"If you're not breaking up with me, what do you call moving back in with your parents?"

Wyatt sighed. "I'm taking a break from you until you come down off your high horse and start acting like yourself again."

Grace thought Wyatt was overacting, but she didn't dare tell him that. "You didn't have to move out. We can work on our problems together. Surely, you'd rather be with me than sleeping in your childhood bedroom."

"I'm not the one with the problem, Grace. And I'm not sleeping in my old bedroom. I'm staying in the guest cottage. My parents are in Europe, and I have the house to myself."

Did she know her future in-laws were in Europe? Grace couldn't remember.

On his end, she heard a door open, followed by music and loud voices. "It sounds like you're having a party," she said.

"Some of the guys came over. We're sitting by the pool."

When a girl squealed in the background, Grace said, "That didn't sound like a guy to me."

"That's Bobby's new girlfriend."

A pang of jealousy darted her heart. "I'm coming home on Sunday. Can we have dinner and talk about this?"

He hesitated, and someone at the party said in a loud voice, "Hey, Wyatt, we need to order some more beer."

"You should tend to your guests," Grace said.

"Right. Dinner on Sunday sounds good. I need to get the rest of my stuff from the house anyway."

Her throat thickened, and tears threatened. "I'll pick up some steaks on my way home from the airport."

"Okay. I'll see you Sunday."

Ending the call, she dumped the rest of her tea in the pool and went inside to her grandfather's study. She dropped two ice cubes into a lowball glass and filled it halfway with his expensive whiskey.

Grace took the drink outside to the rockers on the terrace. She realized her mistake too late. Seated next to her was Crying Susan.

Since there was no way to escape without being rude, Grace struck up a conversation with her. "I've been watching you for the past couple of days. You should leave him, you know?" What was Grace thinking? She was advising a total stranger to leave her cheating husband while she kept a secret to prevent her mother from divorcing her father over his affair with her best friend.

Susan sniffled as she bobbed her head. "You're right. I should. But I can't. He's my whole life. I have no career and no money of my own. My friends are his friends' wives. They will take sides with him in the divorce."

Grace cocked an eyebrow. "Even though he's the one who's been cheating on you?"

Susan stared down at her lap. "Freddy's the life of the party. Everyone overlooks his faults because he's so much fun."

"It sounds like you need new friends. And maybe a fresh start. Surely you can find a job. It doesn't have to be a career. You could work part-time in a boutique or something. You're surrounded by your family this weekend. Won't they support you?"

"I guess so." Susan sobbed into her balled fist. "I just can't let him go. I love him too much."

Grace wondered if her mother loved her father enough to forgive his indiscretions, but she wasn't willing to risk her wedding to find out.

sixteen

· · ·

Kate was tying her tennis shoes early Saturday morning when there was a light tapping on the cottage door. She was taken aback to see her husband standing in the doorway.

He brushed past her into the cottage. "What's going on, Kate? I just left the hospital. According to the admissions desk, Izzy hasn't been admitted since her initial stroke in early June. Where is she?"

Kate's mind raced. She never dreamed her husband would actually come to the Lowcountry. She wondered what Blossom would advise her to do in this situation. She could almost hear the woman say, "Tell the truth, love bug. He will find out soon enough anyway."

"She's asleep," Kate said, gesturing at her mother's closed bedroom door.

The lines on Rand's forehead deepened. "I don't understand. So she didn't have another stroke? She's not on death's doorstep?"

Kate's face warmed. "She's perfectly healthy. Getting stronger every day."

Rand appeared even more confused. "Why did you lie to me?"

"Because it was the only way to get your attention." Kate

pulled out her phone and scrolled down their message thread. "You reached out to me about house-related stuff, but you've ignored me when I've texted you." She clicked on the Phone app. "And I've left you a half dozen voice messages throughout the past few weeks. You didn't answer a single one."

Rand looked from the phone to Kate. "I wasn't intentionally ignoring you if that's what you're suggesting. I figured you were busy taking care of your mother. Wasn't that the purpose of you being here?"

Kate crossed her arms over her chest. "Don't turn this on me. Obviously, you haven't missed me."

"Of course, I've missed you. But I've been busy at the hospital."

A sleepy Grace emerged from their shared bedroom. When she saw her father, she froze. "What're you doing here?"

Rand glanced over at Kate, who shook her head slightly, imploring silently for him not to rat her out. "I came to see my girls. I wanted to surprise you."

"How'd you get here so early? Did you fly in last night?" Grace asked, closing the distance between them.

"Late last night. I got a room at a hotel by the Charleston airport."

"Well, you wasted your time. Mom and I are coming home tomorrow."

"Really?" Rand looked to Kate for confirmation, and she nodded. "Oh, well. At least I'll have one day on the beach. I can fly home with you tomorrow."

"Guess again," Grace said. "According to Shelby, the Nazi reservationist, there are no available rooms in the inn."

His gaze shifted to Kate. "Can't I sleep with you?"

Kate shook her head. "Sorry. Grace and I are sharing a twin-bedded room."

Grace finger-combed her blonde hair back into an elastic band. "You can have my bed. I may drive to Charleston this afternoon and spend the night. I have my rental car. There's no point in staying. I've had enough of Magnolia Shores."

"Let's talk to Shelby first," Kate suggested. "Maybe a guest is checking out early. I can't remember the last time we spent any quality time together as a family, just the four of us. We could spend the day on the beach and have dinner in town."

Grace snorted. "With Shelby? No thanks. The thought of spending the night in a bougie hotel in Charleston is growing quickly on me."

"We don't have to decide right now. I need to start breakfast." Kate looked up at her husband. "Are you hungry?"

"Not really. But I could use some coffee."

"Me too," Grace added. "Since I'm obviously not getting any more sleep."

They waited for Grace to dress before walking across the courtyard to the kitchen. Grace searched the cabinets for to-go cups while Kate counted scoops of coffee into the percolator.

Blossom bustled into the kitchen with Jolene on her heels. "Good morning!" She gave Rand the once over. "Who're you?"

"Blossom, meet my husband, Rand. Rand, this is Blossom."

Mischief filled Blossom's face. "So you're Rand, the mighty heart surgeon and lifesaver. I was beginning to think you were a myth."

Grace rolled her eyes as she filled the cups with coffee. "Let's go down to the beach, Dad. We need to get out of the kitchen so Mom and Blossom can fix breakfast," she said, motioning her father to the door.

Blossom watched them leave before taking her turn at the percolator. "Well, now. How do you like them apples?"

"What apples?" Kate asked, placing mini quiches on a baking sheet.

"Your husband's unexpected visit."

Kate slid the baking sheet into the oven to warm. "His unexpected visit proves my point. He's after my inheritance. The minute he thinks Mom's on death's doorstep, he jumps on a plane and flies to South Carolina."

"Maybe he was worried about *you*. Not your money. I caution you about jumping to conclusions, Katie girl."

Kate cut her eyes at Blossom. "So now you're taking his side?"

"I'm playing devil's advocate. Why not give your marriage one last try? If it doesn't work out, you can file for separation and move on with your life with a clear conscience."

"Hmm," Kate said, tugging at her chin in thought. "Maybe you're right. After thirty years, I guess we owe each other that much."

"Exactly. And who knows? You might discover you still have chemistry. Since you're both here, why not plan a romantic dinner for him?"

Kate opened the oven door to peek at the quiches. "Actually, I was thinking we'd take the girls to town for dinner. We haven't had a family outing in years."

"Even better. Maybe you can carve out some time alone with Rand this afternoon. Take a long walk on the beach, maybe pack a picnic lunch."

"I guess we could do that." Kate hadn't seen her husband in weeks, yet the thought of spending time with him soured her stomach.

Grace and Rand sat in silence at a table by the pool as they checked messages on their phones.

"Did you tell your mom about Claudia and me?" Rand asked.

Grace's head shot up. "No! Claudia warned me to keep our encounter in the kitchen a secret. She wasn't even going to tell you. Why'd she change her mind?"

"She felt guilty. And she wanted me to be prepared to do damage control." Her father sat back in his chair and ran his hand over his balding head. "I don't understand. Why would your mom lie to me if she doesn't know about Claudia?"

Grace furrowed her brow. "What did she lie to you about?"

"She told me Izzy had another stroke and wasn't expected to live. That's why I came."

"That's strange. She wouldn't lie to you about something so important without good reason."

"It's my fault. I've been so busy at work, I've been avoiding her. So, we're keeping this thing with Claudia between us, right? I see no point in upsetting your mom over a meaningless hookup, as you young people call it."

Grace glared at him from beneath her furrowed brow. "Next time you decide to have a meaningless hookup, pick someone other than Mom's best friend."

He nodded curtly. "Point taken. But there won't be a next time."

"I hope not. A messy divorce would put a damper on my wedding. Our big day will be here soon. I can't wait for you to walk me down the aisle," she said in a brighter tone.

His smile didn't quite reach his eyes.

Why the lack of enthusiasm? Grace wondered. She and Rand had been planning her wedding day since she was a little girl. Was he afraid her mom would find out about Claudia? Or was there something else bothering him?

The way things stood with Wyatt, Grace wasn't even sure there would be a wedding. Feeling an urgent need to get home to her fiancé, she picked up her phone and searched the internet for flight schedules.

"What're you doing?" her father asked.

"I'm booking an afternoon flight out of Charleston. I'm tired of sitting around. There's nothing to do here. I don't see why Shelby and Mom love this place so much. You can have my bed."

"No way! I'm going with you. Book two seats, and I'll pay you back."

She looked up at him. "Seriously? But you just got here."

"I came because I was concerned about Izzy. Now that I know she's fine, I need to get back to my patients."

Grace suspected he was lying. He rarely worked on the weekend. But she booked his seat anyway.

Her phone pinged with the confirmation email, and she double-checked the details. "The flight leaves at one, and we arrive in Austin at four thirty." Another email popped into her inbox, and she narrowed her eyes as she read it. "This is odd."

"What is it? A problem with the flights?"

Grace shook her head. "I used Mom's debit card for the band deposit and got a notification saying the charge was declined." She pushed back from the table. "I should tell Mom."

Her father grabbed her arm. "That can wait. We'll have to hurry to make our flights. You can text her on the way to the airport."

She studied her father. Something was definitely off about him. "You're probably right. She'll be mad enough when she finds out we're leaving."

Shelby was returning from a run on the beach when she heard her father's voice. Spotting him sitting with Grace at a table by the pool, she ducked into the sand dunes and crept up as close as she dared.

While Shelby could tell his tone was serious, she was too far away to hear what he was saying. They were conspiring about something. They mentioned Claudia. What does her mother's best friend have to do with anything? As usual, Grace changed the subject to her wedding.

Shelby glanced around her. She was trapped in the dunes, and she couldn't make her presence known without outing herself for spying on them. She sat down in the sand to wait, drawing her knees to her chest. She heard mention of airline tickets. They were leaving today. *Yay!*

When they got up from the table, Shelby followed them into the kitchen. She watched the scene unfold from inside the doorway, listening to her father and sister make excuses about flying home this afternoon instead of waiting to travel with Kate tomorrow morning. Shelby could tell something wasn't right. Why couldn't her father look her mother in the eye? She had an unsettling feeling Grace and Dad were keeping something important from her mother.

"If I get home this afternoon, I'll have all day tomorrow to get organized for the week," Grace explained.

"And since all the rooms are booked, I might as well go with her," Dad said with a shrug.

Her mother's face went dark. "You can sleep in Grace's bed since she's leaving."

Dad's fingers grazed her mom's arm. "I came to check on Izzy. Now that I know she's okay, I should get back to my patients." He glanced at his watch. "Let's go, Grace. We're cutting it close on time."

Shelby waved at her father on his way out the door. "Good to see you, Dad. Thanks for stopping by."

"Oh, Shelby! I didn't notice you standing there." He pressed his cheek to hers. "You're looking well. Good to see you too, sweetheart."

Once they were gone, Kate said to Blossom, "That settles that."

Shelby's head swiveled back and forth between Blossom and her mother. "That settles what?"

"Nothing, sweetheart. I'm just disappointed we didn't have any family time together." Kate came around the island to Shelby. "But I won't let them ruin my last day here. What are your plans for today? Can you spare some time for your mom?"

Shelby smiled. "Of course. I'm working the desk, but I can take breaks. What did you have in mind?"

"I need to finish up with breakfast and start packing, which will take some time since my stuff is strewn all over the place. We could have lunch by the pool, maybe sit on the beach for a while."

"That sounds great," Shelby said.

"Then it's a date. Now, excuse me while I check on our guests," Kate said, disappearing into the dining room.

Blossom whispered to Shelby, "Your mom could use some perking up. What do you think about throwing her a surprise going-away party?"

Shelby's face lit up. "I love that idea! We can invite Pritchard and Savannah. Maybe Harper and Cody too."

"We can't forget Izzy and Silas. If you invite the others and set the table, I'll go to the market and cook."

"Deal," Shelby said, offering Blossom a high five.

Blossom opened a can of dog food and dumped it into a bowl. "How was your date with Josh last night."

"It was good. Really good, actually," Shelby said with a dreamy expression. "Wait a minute. I don't remember telling you his name."

Blossom flashed her a mischievous grin. "You should know by now that I have a way of finding these things out. So, you like this young man?"

"I do." Shelby made a glass of ice water and sat down at the table. "But I feel differently about him than I did about Luke and Matt. And that confuses me."

"How so?" Blossom asked, lowering herself to a chair opposite Shelby.

"In hindsight, I stayed with Luke out of habit. We'd been together since middle school, and I didn't know how to live without him."

Blossom nodded. "Breaking habits is difficult."

"Exactly. The chemistry between Matt and me is smoking hot." Shelby's face warmed. "Sorry, I probably shouldn't say that to an angel."

Blossom chuckled. "You can say anything to me, baby girl. There is nothing I haven't heard before."

"I don't doubt that," Shelby said, tracing the rim of her water glass. "Should I be worried that I don't feel that same burning desire with Josh? I'm attracted to him. I certainly enjoy kissing him. He's easy to be with and fun to talk to."

"Every relationship is a journey, a unique path carved by the hearts of two people," Blossom said in a wise voice. "Burning passion is intoxicating, but it often fizzles over time. Seek the man who cherishes your quirks, celebrates your strengths, and loves you unconditionally, flaws and all. Find the guy with staying power who will always support you in your many endeavors."

Shelby nodded, afraid to speak for fear she might cry. She had a tall order to fill in finding a man like Blossom described.

seventeen

. . .

Grace stopped by the gourmet market on her way home from the airport and purchased her husband's favorite snacks and a bottle of Chandon Champagne. When she arrived home, she quickly unpacked, showered, and dressed in her rose-colored romper with the super-short shorts that drove Wyatt crazy. She packed a picnic in a wicker basket and drove the short distance to his parents' house. Parking in the driveway, she followed the loud music to the backyard, where she found her fiancé sitting alone on the edge of the pool, his head bowed and feet dangling in the water.

When she called his name, he looked up, waved, and dropped his gaze back to the pool. Not the homecoming greeting she'd hoped for. She had more work cut out for her than she realized.

She set the basket on the pool deck and kicked off her sandals. When she sat down next to him, she got a whiff of sweat and booze. Waving her hand in front of her nose, she said, "Woo wee. Must have been some party last night. Why the gloomy mood?"

"The party got out of hand. My parents' house was trashed. I've been cleaning up all day. I don't want to live the bachelor life, Grace."

"You don't have to, babe. We can figure this out. The wedding is the only thing we argue about. Aside from that, we get along great."

"But the wedding is a *big* thing." He raked his fingers through his hair. "Not only are you obsessed with every little wedding detail, you demand to be the center of attention all the time. You're not the only woman who ever got married."

Irritation ruffled the hairs on the back of her neck. "I'm aware of that, Wyatt. But I only plan to get married once, and I want our wedding to be special. What's so wrong with that?"

He pressed his hand against his head as though his brain hurt. "Because you've taken things too far. What if you don't come down off this cloud after the wedding? You're unbearable to be around. You've turned into a real Diva-zilla. Our marriage won't survive."

Ouch. A Diva-zilla? Am I that bad? "I love you with my whole heart, Wyatt. And I want to make our relationship work. I'm open to suggestions."

He looked at her with a bemused expression, seemingly surprised she asked for his opinion. "In that case, I suggest we have a small wedding with only our families and a few friends."

A few friends? Grace had planned to invite the entire town. Her mind raced. She was not yet ready to give up her big wedding. "Why don't we compromise?"

"Compromise how?" Wyatt asked in a disgruntled tone.

"I'm not sure. Let's have some Champagne and talk about it." She dragged the picnic basket closer and removed the Champagne, giving Wyatt the bottle to open. She filled two glasses, but when she handed him one, he shook his head.

"No thanks. After last night, I'm on the wagon for a while."

"Are you hungry? I brought your favorite goat cheese." She opened the container of cheese spread and a package of thin wheat crackers.

She sipped Champagne, and he snacked on the cheese and crackers while they discussed options for their wedding. They considered changing the venue or having a small destination wedding.

"I don't know, Wyatt. If we cancel our original plans, my parents will lose a lot of money on deposits." Grace was stretching the truth. The only nonrefundable deposit was for the band, and that charge had been declined. Realizing she'd forgotten to tell her mom about the declined charge, she quickly thumbed off a text.

"Who are you texting?" Wyatt asked suspiciously.

"My mom. I left my flip-flops by the pool at Magnolia Shores, and I asked her to grab them for me." She set her phone down and poured herself more Champagne. "Let's try a different approach. What if we stick with the original wedding plans but make a pact not to discuss the wedding at all? I'll even sacrifice the professional fireworks display and getaway helicopter." Her mother had nixed those suggestions anyway.

"I don't think you can do it."

"For the sake of our relationship, I most certainly can." Grace dragged an imaginary zipper across her lips. "Mum's the word. No more wedding talk." She walked her fingers up his arm to his neck, toying with the wave of dark hair behind his ear. "If you move back in with me, I'll prove myself to you. I promise you won't be sorry."

Wyatt shook his head. "I'm not ready to move back in yet."

"What if I stay here with you, then? With your parents away, we'll have the place to ourselves, and we can pretend we're at summer camp. The change of scenery will help us get out of our rut. We can swim naked in the pool, and no one will even see us," she said, sweeping an arm at the lush foliage surrounding the pool.

The bulge in his shorts told her he liked this idea.

She moved closer to him. "We could have a romantic dinner tonight. Cook some steaks on the grill. I bought a new sexy negligee I've been saving for a special occasion."

Wyatt slid a hand up her shorts and fingered her lacy thong.

"I'm willing to give it a try, Grace. But I'll kick you out at the first sign of Diva Zilla."

"Understood. I'm putting Diva Zilla back in her cage. Should we run to the store for those steaks?"

"I guess," Wyatt said, apparently still skeptical.

Grace got up and pulled Wyatt to his feet. "And we can stop by the house for my negligee on the way back."

A slow smile spread across his lips. "Now we're talking."

Wyatt insisted on driving since Grace had been drinking Champagne. On the way to the store, he asked, "So, how are things in South Carolina?"

"Good. Izzy's recovering well." She shifted in her seat toward him. "Oh! I almost forgot. You're not going to believe this. My dad is having an affair with Claudia."

Wyatt's brown eyes grew wide. "Your mom's best friend Claudia?"

"Yep," she said and filled him in on everything that had happened with Claudia and her father.

"How did your mom take the news when you told her?"

Grace bit her lower lip. Since she had promised not to mention their wedding, she couldn't very well reveal the real reason she'd kept her father's affair from her mother. "I didn't tell her. I'm not even sure they're actually having an affair. Dad and Claudia both swear it was a one-night thing."

"And you believed them?"

"I don't know what to think, honestly. I wish I knew for certain."

"There must be a way for you to find out," he said, turning his right blinker on as they approached the grocery store.

Grace sat up straight in her seat. "Actually, there is. I have an idea. Don't turn here. Go straight," she said, jabbing a finger at the windshield and the road ahead.

He turned off his blinker and continued driving down the road. "What're you thinking, Grace? Where are we going?"

"To my parents' house. Mom is coming home tomorrow. If

Dad and Claudia are in a relationship, they will be together tonight."

He glared at her over the top of his sunglasses. "And? Are you suggesting we spy on them?"

Grace bobbed her head, her ponytail skimming her shoulders. "Yep! That's the idea."

As they approached her family's home, she spotted her father's car in the driveaway. "Good! Dad's here. If my hunch is right, Claudia's car is hidden in the garage." As Wyatt parked alongside the curb, Grace opened the car door. "Wait here. I'll be right back."

"Hold on! You're not going anywhere without me," he said, killing the engine and hurrying after her.

They sprinted to the garage and peered through the window at the old minivan. "I was right. That's Claudia's van," Grace said under her breath to Wyatt.

When she took off around the side of the house, Wyatt caught up with her, grabbing her elbow to stop her. "Wait, Grace. You need a plan. You can't just go barging in on them. What if they're . . . you know?"

"Having sex? I'm counting on it." She flashed her phone at him. "I need evidence to show Mom when I break the news to her."

"Are you sure about this, Grace?"

"I'm positive," she said, using her key to unlock the kitchen door.

When they entered the house, they heard soft music and low voices wafting from down the hall. "They're in the family room," Grace whispered.

"Yeah. But they may not be having sex. What if they're watching a movie?"

"Only one way to find out." Grace hugged the wall as she inched down the hall to the family room, peeking around the doorjamb.

Grace was unprepared to see Claudia straddling her father on the sofa. She shrunk back in shock, pressing her body against the wall. "I'm gonna be sick. Here, you do it." She handed Wyatt her phone and fled the house through the back door.

She was in the car, gulping in deep breaths of air and forcing back the urge to vomit, when Wyatt came running around the side of the house. He handed her the phone. "Here's your evidence."

Grace dropped her phone in her lap without looking at the pictures. "Did they see you?"

"Not a chance. They were too interested in each other to notice me." Wyatt put the car in gear and sped away from the curb.

Grace closed her eyes and rested her head against the seat as she tried to erase the mental image of her father and Claudia naked.

"What're you going to do? This isn't the kind of news you break over the phone. Will you fly back to the Lowcountry?"

"That's not necessary. My mom is coming home tomorrow. But I have no clue how to tell her about this."

Wyatt cut his eyes at Grace. "But you *are* going to tell her, aren't you?"

"Of course, I'm going to tell her. Duh." Truthfully, Grace had no clue what she'd do. She would think long and hard before she made her next move.

eighteen

· · ·

K ate finished packing and set out her clothes for tomorrow. She would need to leave before dawn to make it to the Charleston airport in time for her flight. Slipping her feet into her flip-flops, she wandered over to the main house in search of Shelby. She worried Pritchard was stretching her daughter too thin. Shelby was awfully young and inexperienced to be burdened with the responsibility of managing the B&B. And now, in Kate's absence, Shelby would have the added duty of serving breakfast to their guests. However, since they were planning to shut down during construction, there was no point in hiring new staff.

She dreaded saying goodbye to her precious youngest daughter. They'd grown close these past few weeks, and she would miss her as much as she would miss the Lowcountry. But she needed to go home to confront her husband about their marriage problems.

The house was quiet. Most of their guests had gone to town for dinner. Shelby wasn't seated at her desk, but she heard voices outside on the patio. Emerging through the French doors, she noticed a small group of her family and friends gathered near the pool. When they saw her, they let out a chorus of surprise.

"What's all this?" Kate asked as she closed the distance between them.

Shelby placed a tumbler with a reddish-orange beverage in her hand. "We're having a going-away party for you. It was Blossom's idea, of course."

Kate smiled over at the exotic woman. "Of course." She sipped the beverage. "This is delicious. What's in it?"

"Vodka, peach schnapps, orange juice, cranberry juice, and a splash of grenadine. I'm calling it Farewell Sunset." Shelby pressed her cheek to Kate's, whispering, "I'm going to miss you so much, Mama."

Kate gripped her daughter tight with her free arm. "I'm going to miss you, too, sweet girl. But I feel good about leaving you. You've grown up so much since you came here. You have Lowcountry in your blood. You belong at Magnolia Shores."

Shelby nodded, her eyes shiny with unshed tears. "And so do you. This place has a strong hold on you. I have a feeling you won't be gone long."

Kate dropped her hand from her daughter's waist. "We'll see, sweetheart. I can't come back until I sort out my life."

"If you need a job, Pritchard will hire you."

Kate shook her head. "My career isn't the issue."

Shelby narrowed her eyes. "Then what is the issue? Dad? He certainly didn't stay long. It shows how little he wants to spend time with us."

Her daughter's wounded expression tugged at Kate's heartstrings. She was more certain than ever that something was going on with her husband. The old Rand, the considerate man she'd married, would never have treated his family with such disregard. Beautiful nurses threw themselves at him all the time, but she didn't think he was the type to have an affair. It must be something else. She hoped he wasn't ill.

The others joined them, saving Kate from having to respond to Shelby.

Izzy reached for Kate's hand and squeezed. "I'm truly going to miss you, darling. But I'm grateful you stayed as long as you did. I never would have made it through these past difficult weeks without you."

Silas gave her a rare smile. "I'm going to miss you too. I've gotten used to having you around."

Kate chuckled. "You're going to miss my help at the reception desk. If you and Shelby get in over your head, you must promise to call Pritchard for help."

Pritchard's shoulders sagged. "Unfortunately, I'm leaving for Nashville on Monday. I'm not sure how long I'll be gone."

Blossom puffed out her ample chest. "I'll be here. You can count on me to serve breakfast. I'm happy to greet your guests at the door, but I'm not good with computers. All those fancy electronic gadgets came after my time," she said with a belly laugh.

"You're a lifesaver, Blossom. I'm going to have to put you on the payroll," Pritchard said

"That's not necessary." Blossom jabbed him in the side with her elbow. "Just comp my stay."

"Gladly! You're worth the nightly rate and then some."

Blossom shook her head. "I'm just joking. I don't need any handouts. I'm here on a mission. My second mission, actually. If anyone is willing, I'd love a hand in the kitchen, getting dinner on the table."

Everyone except Pritchard and Kate followed her inside. "Where's Savannah tonight?" Kate asked.

"She had to work, but she said to tell you goodbye. She'll miss you, as will we all." Pritchard set his penetrating gaze on her. "How long will you be gone? Will you work a two-week notice after you hand in your resignation?"

"I got fired from my job, Pritchard—demoted, actually. My executive team gave my position to the young woman covering for me during my absence. They realized they could pay her a lot less money." Kate shrugged. "They actually did me a favor. They made my decision to leave easier."

"In that case, I'm glad it worked out. One less thing you have to worry about. Shelby tells me Rand made a brief appearance earlier today."

"Very brief." Kate was too ashamed to admit she'd lied to her husband about their mother's health. "As you know, things aren't great between us."

Pritchard nodded. "Be cautious about your next move, Kate."

His sinister warning made her shiver. "What do you mean?"

"Get legal advice from a reputable divorce attorney before you leave him."

She shook her head in disbelief. "Legal advice? I'm not sure I'm ready for a divorce attorney."

"You seem ready to me. What about your business venture, Lumina Designs?"

Kate massaged her temples. "I'm not sure about anything right now. Magnolia Shores has a powerful hold on me. Once I'm home, I'll be able to think straight."

He pulled her in for a half hug. "I'm here for you, Kate. If you need me, I'll be in Texas in a flash."

"I appreciate that, Pritchard, more than you know," Kate said past the lump in her throat. Divorce seemed so final. If she could determine the problem in her marriage, perhaps she and Rand could fix it. When she got home, she would invite Claudia over for coffee. Her best friend, a big proponent of marriage counseling, offered valuable guidance.

The others emerged from the kitchen with the food—a platter of fried flounder filets, a macaroni and cheese casserole, a big bowl of slaw, and homemade buttermilk biscuits. Dinner was a festive occasion with good wine, delicious food, and a lively discussion about their expansion plans. A light breeze blew off the ocean, and the sky grew orange as the sunset approached. Kate tried to capture the image in her mind for later when she returned home to Texas.

When guests began trickling back from town, Silas and Shelby returned to their workstations. Pritchard walked Izzy to the cottage while Blossom and Kate started on the dishes.

"Can you come home to Texas with me? I need my spiritual advisor," Kate said.

Blossom chuckled. "Sorry, love bug. I have to stay at Magnolia Shores, but I'll be here when you return. If you need me, call the main number and have Shelby put me on the phone."

"Why do you sound so confident I'll be coming back?"

Blossom shrugged. "Just a hunch."

Kate rinsed a serving platter and handed it to Blossom. "Do you have any parting words of wisdom?"

Blossom dried the platter. "Just the tried and true about following your heart. Trust your instincts and embrace the journey, even if it means taking risks or stepping into the unknown."

When they finished with the dishes, Blossom engulfed her in a warm embrace. "Your girls are grown young women, capable of caring for themselves. Now it's time to focus on yourself."

Tears filled Kate's eyes, and she sniffled. "Izzy said something similar the other day."

"Mamas usually know best," Blossom said, pushing Kate away to look at her. "I don't like judging people, especially when I've just met them. But something about your husband rubbed me the wrong way. I have a sneaking suspicion he's hiding something."

Kate swiped at her tears. "I think so too. I just need to determine what it is."

When Kate returned to the cottage, Izzy was already in bed. She'd been so preoccupied with her farewell dinner that she hadn't checked her phone for hours. She frowned as she read Grace's text message about the declined debit charge for the band deposit. How could that be? There was usually plenty of money in their joint account.

Retrieving her laptop from the bedroom, she sat down at the kitchen table and accessed her online banking. Her mouth dropped open when she saw less than a thousand dollars in the account. She couldn't remember the last time she'd checked her balance. All her bills were set up on autopay, and she'd had few incidentals while at Magnolia Shores.

She scrolled through the debits. Over the past month, Rand had made several large transfers to his individual account. Her mind raced as she snapped the laptop shut. But why? Was he having financial problems? How could that be when he'd saved a large percentage of his annual salary for their entire married life? There must be another explanation. Whatever it was, she intended to find out.

nineteen

. . .

Shelby snatched the vibrating phone off her nightstand, answering with a groggy, "Hello."

"Hey, kiddo. What're you doing?"

Shelby cracked an eyelid and waited for her vision to clear to read the clock. "It's midnight, Matt. I'm sleeping. What do you think I'm doing?"

"It's Saturday night. I thought you might be out with your new boyfriend."

Matt's voice sounded off. Was he slurring his words? Had he been drinking? "One date with Josh doesn't make him my boyfriend. Not that it's any of your business, but I've been here all night. We had a farewell dinner for Mom earlier. Why aren't *you* out with your new girlfriend?"

"Ada had to work," he said.

"On Saturday night? Is she a waitress or something?"

"Nah. She's a nurse at the hospital. She takes care of itty-bitty babies."

Shelby's heart sank. Ada was a nurse, probably thirty years old—not a *kiddo* like Shelby. "Good for her. What do you want, Matt? I have breakfast duty in the morning, and I need to sleep."

"I have something really important to ask you."

Shelby rolled over on her back. "Then ask me."

"I can't over the phone. I'm in my boat at your dock. Come down here."

Shelby threw her legs over the side of the bed. What was so crucial for him to come here in his boat at midnight? There was only one way for her to find out. "All right. I'll be down in a minute."

Pulling a sweatshirt over her pajama top, Shelby slipped her feet into flip-flops and left her room. On the dock, she found Matt sitting on the end with shoulders slumped and legs hanging over the side.

She sat down beside him. "What's so important it couldn't wait until tomorrow?"

He looked up at her with bloodshot eyes. "Hey, beautiful."

She waved her hand in front of her nose. "You reek of booze. I thought you didn't drink."

"I only had a teensy bit," he said, demonstrating a small amount with his thumb and pointer finger. "Look at you. You're a smoke show with your wild strawberry hair and sultry green eyes."

"Seriously, Matt. What's your big question?"

Running his fingers through her hair, he cupped the back of her head and pulled her face close. "I can't stop thinking about what happened the other day in the boat," he said, his mouth hovering over hers.

"That was a mistake, Matt. I was furious at my sister. I wasn't thinking straight. It didn't mean anything."

"You're lying. You know, it meant something. You are so hot, Shelby." His mouth clamped down on hers, and he was all over her, one hand up her sweatshirt and the other tugging at her pajama bottoms.

"Matt! Stop!" She pushed him away and scrambled to her feet.

He hugged a piling as he pulled himself up. "Don't be like this, Shelby. You know you want me."

"Not like this. You attacked me just now."

"Like you attacked me on the boat. You can't deny our attraction. We have crazy chemistry. You're so damn beautiful. If you weren't such a temptress," he said, grabbing a handful of her hair.

She yanked his hand away. "Don't touch me. What about Ada? And what about our age difference?"

"None of that matters. I wanna be with you. I don't care how old you are. I think about you all the time, Shelby. You're inside my head, driving me crazy."

"This is a booty call. Nothing else. You won't feel the same tomorrow."

He appeared wounded. "The hell I won't."

"Then come back when you're sober, and we'll talk. Good night, Matt." When she turned away, he stumbled down the dock after her.

"Wait, Shelby. Don't go." He tried to grab her arm and nearly fell into the water.

Shelby held onto him, righting him. "You can't drive your boat in this condition." She pulled out her phone. "I'll call you an Uber," she said, but she knew it was pointless. There were no Ubers available on Sandy Island at midnight.

"Never mind. I'll drive you in my car, and you can come back tomorrow for your boat." When he started to argue, she cut him off. "Seriously, Matt. It's too dangerous. You could get a boating under the influence ticket. Or worse. It's pitch black out. You could run into a dock and kill yourself."

He hung his head. "You're right. I shouldn't be driving. Are you sure you don't mind giving me a ride?"

"Yes, I mind. I'd much rather be sleeping. You owe me one." When they reached the courtyard, she instructed him to wait beside her Wrangler while she went inside for her keys.

They said little on the drive to town. Matt gave her directions, and she pulled into the driveway of a stunning waterfront estate. "You live here?"

"Not me. My parents. This is our family's home. I left my truck here earlier. I'll crash here tonight and have someone bring me back for my boat tomorrow." He flashed her a grin. "Unless you want to help me out."

"You can call me when you get up, but I'll probably be working."

He kissed her cheek. "I meant those things I said earlier. I'll prove it to you tomorrow when I'm sober."

"I'm not holding my breath," Shelby mumbled.

She replayed the exchange on her drive back to Magnolia Shores. Earlier in the summer, Matt had hinted at an addiction problem he suffered several years back. He told her he'd chosen the wrong career path and temporarily lost his way. She hoped he hadn't gone off the wagon.

She couldn't sleep, her mind racing with his words about their chemistry and her being inside his head. Would he repeat those things when he returned for his boat tomorrow? Would he even remember? She drifted off to sleep, imagining him professing his love for her. But around ten on Sunday morning, she was helping a guest load luggage into their trunk when a fancy red sports car with Ada behind the wheel drove into the courtyard. Matt exited the passenger side and darted toward the dock without so much as a glance in Shelby's direction.

twenty

· · ·

K ate arrived home from the airport midafternoon on Sunday to find Rand watching a golf tournament in the family room, the lights out and drapes drawn against the summer sun.

"You're home," he said unenthusiastically when she entered the room.

Throwing open the drapes, she grabbed the remote from the coffee table and clicked off the television. "What happened to the money in our joint account?"

He let out a deep sigh. "You'd better sit down."

Her heart skipped a beat as she lowered herself to the edge of the sofa beside him. "What's going on, Rand? You're scaring me."

He leaned forward, elbows on knees and fingers intertwined. "A few years ago, I invested my savings in a revolutionary medical device that utilized advanced sensors and AI algorithms to detect and manage heart conditions in real time. The device had enormous potential, with projected returns of twenty to thirty times my initial investment. Unfortunately, the project was terribly mismanaged, and I lost everything," he says as tears welled in his eyes.

Kate's stomach lurched, and she thought she might be sick. In the thirty years they'd been married, she had never seen her husband cry, not even happy tears over the birth of their daughters.

He swiped angrily at his eyes. "I'm so sorry, honey. I had big plans to retire early and buy you a vacation home in Florida and the sport fishing boat I've always dreamed of. Now I'll have to work well into my sixties to compensate for the lost savings."

Kate's thoughts whirled as she tried to comprehend the implications of their new financial status. "By *savings*, does that include the money you set aside for Grace's wedding?"

He nodded, unable to meet her gaze. "Sadly."

Kate shook her head in confusion. "But I don't understand. You earn a substantial salary. Why did you empty our joint account?"

He lowered his gaze to the floor. "There's more. I didn't just invest our savings. I also took out a home equity loan. I used the money in our joint account to make a payment."

Kate blinked hard. "*A* payment? You mean there are more payments due?"

He nodded, staring down at the floor. "Several more. We'll have to sell the house."

Kate shot off the sofa like a rocket. "So, I was right. You were after my inheritance."

He looked up at her, his face registering surprise. "I certainly didn't wish for Izzy to die. But her death would've been timely." Rand stood to face her. "I'm so sorry, Kate. I know I've disappointed you." He took her by the arms. "I realize things aren't great between us, but I think we should get marriage counseling. If you give me another chance, I'd like to try and make it up to you."

"Why now, Rand? I've asked you many times over the years to seek counseling."

"This failed investment has been a reality check for me. I've been assessing my life, and I realize I've done wrong by you on so many levels," he said, no longer trying to hide his tears.

Kate's heart went out to him. He seemed so lost, so desolate. Admitting his mistakes could not be easy for a man with his ego.

He dried his eyes with the hem of his polo shirt. "Can I interest you in a romantic dinner? We could cook steaks on the grill and open a bottle of red wine. We can talk, really talk, like we used to."

Kate's brow shot up. "Can you afford steaks?"

Rand forced a smile. "Hot dogs and baked beans, then?"

"I can't think about food right now. I'm going to unpack," she said and fled the room.

Kate made multiple trips up and down the stairs, bringing her luggage in from the car. Rand, who had returned to watching golf on television, didn't offer to help. If he wanted to salvage what was left of their marriage, he had a funny way of showing it.

After unpacking her suitcases, Kate came back downstairs to find the family room empty and Rand's car missing from the driveway. She roamed nervously around the house like a caged animal. She longed to be back at Magnolia Shores. While the cottage she shared with Izzy was tiny, every window offered a sweeping view of the inlet and ocean.

She ate cereal for dinner and watched *The Notebook* on television, a heartwarming tale of love and memory loss starring Ryan Gosling and Rachel McAdams. Kate had married Rand for better or worse. How could she leave him now, when he was down and out? But she was so disappointed in him. How would she ever get over his betrayal?

She pretended to be asleep when Rand climbed into bed beside her around midnight. A sweet floral scent clung to him, definitely not his bergamot aftershave. She waited until she heard his soft snores before slipping out of bed and going downstairs. She was still sitting at the kitchen table, a cup of cold coffee in front of her, when he came down at seven on Monday morning.

"What happened to our romantic dinner last night?" she asked.

"I had to check on a couple of patients and got hung up at the hospital." He glanced at his watch. "And I have an early surgery this morning. I'll bring home dinner tonight, and we'll have that talk." He leaned over to kiss her cheek. "I love you, Kate. I don't want to lose you."

Kate didn't respond. She already felt lost to him.

The long day loomed ahead of her. How would she spend her time without a job? She texted Claudia.

Are you up for a walk? I could use a friend.

Claudia responded immediately.

Sure! I'll meet you at the park in ten.

Racing up the stairs, Kate brushed her teeth and changed into exercise clothes. She was waiting on the swings at the playground down the street when her best friend arrived.

Since Kate had last seen her weeks ago, Claudia had lightened her hair and lost weight. She'd struggled with depression after her youngest left for college. With her husband frequently away on business trips, she'd often complained of boredom, but she refused to find a new hobby or get a part-time job.

Kate jumped off the swing to her feet. "You look amazing, girlfriend. What gives? Did Bobby get a new job that doesn't require travel?"

Claudia appeared confused at first and then let out a fake laugh. "Nope. He's been gone more than ever." She chewed on her lower lip. "So what's the major crisis? Why do you need a friend?"

Kate puffed out her chest, summoning the courage to say the words for the first time. "Rand has put the final nail in the coffin of our marriage."

Claudia stiffened. "What makes you say that?"

"He cleared out our joint account without my permission."

Claudia listened with a straight face as Kate gave a brief overview of Rand's failed investment.

"I agree that's bad, Kate. But it could be worse."

"How? He neglected to tell me about this business venture. And now we're broke. We don't even have the money for Grace's wedding."

Claudia went rigid at the mention of Kate's daughter. "I'm so sorry to hear that. How is Grace, by the way? Have you seen her lately?"

"She spent a few days with me in South Carolina. She's the same old Grace. Self-centered as always."

"That's good. Let's walk," Claudia said and started down their usual path on the sidewalk.

Kate frowned at Claudia's retreating back. What does that mean? *That's good.* Something about Claudia was off today.

Kate hurried to catch up with her friend. "So, what do you think I should do about Rand?"

"Leave him," Claudia deadpanned.

Kate scoffed. "Are you joking? You're the biggest advocate for couples counseling that I know."

Claudia glanced sideways at her. "But he stole your money. How could you ever trust him again?"

"The money was in a joint account. It belonged to both of us." Why was she defending her husband? Kate would never have taken the money without asking Rand first.

"And he took your half without asking. In my book, that makes him a thief."

"Come on, Claudia. We both know he's not a thief. He took the money because he was in a bind. I kinda feel sorry for him. He actually cried yesterday when he told me. He made a bad investment. He's not a gambling addict or anything like that."

They stopped at an intersection, waiting for a line of traffic to pass. Claudia turned to face her. "Have you looked at yourself in the mirror lately? You're glowing from head to toe. Your time in South Carolina restored you. Your marriage has been on the rocks for years. Sell your house, pay off the debt, and go your separate ways."

The traffic passed, and they crossed the intersection. Tears blurred Kate's vision as she stared down at the sidewalk. "I'm not sure I'm ready for such a big move. Divorce is so permanent. I don't want to grow old alone."

"Ha! Who said anything about growing old alone? Within a year, you'll be having hot sex with some gorgeous southern man." Claudia looped her arm through Kate's. "Don't get me wrong, girlfriend. I will miss you terribly. But I wouldn't encourage you to leave him if I didn't believe in my heart that this is the right thing for you."

They walked arm in arm in silence, each lost in her own thoughts. When they parted at the playground with a hug, Kate got a whiff of her intoxicating perfume. "Are you wearing a new scent?" she asked, pulling away

"Yes! Do you like it?" Claudia smelled the inside of her wrist. "It's called Enchanted Garden."

"It's lovely. It smells like jasmine." Her tone grew serious. "Thanks for the pep talk, Claud. I don't know what I'd do without you."

"You'll be fine. You're a survivor." Claudia took Kate's hands in hers. "Regardless of what happens, you're the best friend a girl could ever have."

Kate smiled. "Right back at you."

Claudia turned and headed off in the opposite direction. As she watched her friend disappear around a corner, an ominous feeling overtook Kate. She sensed that everything in her life was about to change, including her relationship with her closest and oldest friend.

Back at home, Kate took a long shower, wrapped herself in a towel, and flipped through the hanging clothes in her walk-in closet. She considered going to work. She felt confident that senior management would hire her as a sales associate. She could easily make up for the salary cut with commissions. With dual incomes,

Kate and Rand would be back on solid financial ground in no time. They could buy a condominium in an adult residential community and seek counseling to rekindle their relationship.

The enormity of her situation overwhelmed her, and she cautioned herself against making any drastic decisions about her future. She turned out the closet light and went into the bedroom. Exhausted from her sleepless night, she dropped her towel and slipped between the cool, crisp sheets. She fell asleep before her head hit the pillow.

twenty-one

· · ·

Shelby was eating an egg salad sandwich at her desk early Monday afternoon when Pritchard stuck his head in the front door.

Surprised to see him, Shelby said, "I thought you were in Nashville."

"I postponed my trip until Wednesday to have a preliminary construction meeting with Will. He's outside now if you care to join us."

"Sure! Be there in a second." She stuffed the last bite of sandwich into her mouth and hurried out the front door. The sight of Matt standing with Will and Pritchard in the courtyard stopped her dead in her tracks on the stoop.

Will motioned for her to join them. "Hey, Shelby. Have you met Matt? He'll be the project manager on the new building."

"We've met." Shelby's stomach knotted as she continued down the steps toward them. As project manager, she would have to work with him every day. She reminded herself she was a professional, and her family owning Magnolia Shores gave her the upper hand.

"Our goal is to have everything in place in order to begin digging footings the day after Labor Day," Will explained.

Shelby smiled. "That's exciting. I can't believe this is actually happening."

Will chuckled. "You'll believe it when we bring in the earthmovers. The surveyor will be out to stake the building this week," he said, and the foursome strolled over to the building site.

Excitement flickered across Shelby's chest as she listened carefully to the men discussing the construction process. She would take advantage of every learning opportunity associated with this project.

When Pritchard pulled Will aside to discuss finances, Matt and Shelby walked back toward the main house.

"I'm sorry about Saturday night," Matt said.

Shelby cut her eyes at him. "You mean about your booty call?"

A flush crept up Matt's neck. "Did I hit on you? I don't remember much. Did you give me a ride home?"

"Yep. I couldn't let you drive the boat in your condition. What got into you? I thought you didn't drink?"

Matt stuffed his hands in his pockets, shifting his weight nervously. "I'm not sure, honestly. I went out with some friends. One beer led to a few too many. It was a harsh reminder of why I quit drinking. I apologize if I said anything inappropriate."

Shelby grunted. "The entire exchange was inappropriate."

"I truly am sorry, Shelby." Matt lowered his voice and leaned in close. "Do you think we could keep this between us? Will is giving me the opportunity to prove myself by managing The Sanctuary project. I don't want him to be concerned that I have a drinking problem."

"This project means a lot to me too, Matt. I won't say anything as long as nothing like that happens again."

"It won't! I promise," he said, tracing a cross over his heart with his finger.

Matt seemed more concerned about his job than Ada. Maybe they were no longer seeing each other. "Are you and Ada still together? I wasn't sure, considering the way you came on to me.

Ashley Farley

"We're still dating. She was working Saturday night. I wouldn't want Ada to know about my moment of weakness. She and I have a lot in common. We're a good fit."

Shelby's anger surged. "How so? Because she's a nurse? Or because she's closer to your age than I am?"

Noticing Pritchard and Will coming toward them, Matt said, "I can see you're still upset. Let's talk about this later."

"Let's not. Consider the whole thing forgotten." Shelby smiled at her uncle as Pritchard approached them. "I need to get back inside, but I have a date tonight. Since you're not leaving for Nashville until Wednesday, is there any chance you could cover the desk for me?"

"Of course, Shelby. I'd be happy to," Pritchard said.

She turned to Will. "I'm looking forward to working with you. I'm usually around if you need anything."

Will nodded. "I'll keep that in mind. Great to see you, Shelby."

Shelby turned her back on the threesome without uttering a word to Matt. She felt his eyes burning her back as she entered the house. If he wanted to play games, so could she.

Josh had texted Shelby earlier that morning, inviting her to dinner, but she hadn't responded yet. She'd been holding on to a glimmer of hope that Matt had meant what he'd said on Saturday night about her being inside his head and driving him crazy. Clearly, he'd been lying.

Back at her desk, she texted Josh.

> Sorry for the delayed response. I needed to get someone to cover for me at work. I would love to have dinner with you.

Why not have dinner with Josh? Even if he didn't make her heart flutter, he was a nice guy with a lot going for him. And he could help her forget about Matt.

138

Kate startled awake from her long nap, her heart pounding as her dream rushed back to her. She was in an enchanted garden, following the scent of jasmine through the boxwood maze. Shadowy figures lurked around every corner—a man and woman kissing, although she couldn't make out their faces. What was the significance of the dream? Did she know the man and woman in the lover's embrace?

Peeling back the bed covers, she was shocked to find herself naked. She never slept in the buff, but exhaustion had left her too drained to put on her nightgown. She retrieved her robe from the bathroom door and slipped it on. The fragrance of jasmine engulfed her. Claudia's new perfume. Was it the same scent she smelled on Rand last night? Kate shivered as a chill crawled across her skin. Are her husband and best friend having an affair?

Soundbites from her conversation with Claudia that morning echoed in her mind. *Leave him. Your marriage has been on the rocks for years. Sell your house, pay off the debt, and go your separate ways. You'll be fine. You're a survivor. Regardless of what happens, you're the best friend a girl could ever have.*

Claudia talked as though the breakup of both their friendship and Kate's marriage was imminent. Throwing her head back, she let out a bellow of rage. Was this really happening? How could she have been such a fool? But what if she was wrong? She needed evidence.

She dressed in the first clothes she could find—denim cutoff shorts and an old cotton T-shirt—and began tearing the room apart. In Rand's blue sport coat pocket, she discovered a lipstick matching Claudia's brand and color. She found a historical romance novel by Claudia's favorite author in the top drawer of her nightstand. And under their bed near the headboard, she unearthed a black lacey thong. Whether or not the panties belonged to Claudia, they were definitely not Kate's.

Kate's search of the rest of the house proved clean until she ransacked Rand's study. She found nothing in his bookshelves or drawers. But his Message app on his iMac computer yielded a gold mine. She knew his passcode. He hadn't even bothered to change it. It was as though he'd wanted her to find the naked photos and vulgar text messages he and Claudia had been exchanging for more than two years. *Two years!*

Kate fell back in her chair as the dam burst and tears streamed down her face. She'd lost everything—her marriage, her best friend, her home. Not to mention the money she'd contributed to their joint savings account and the job she'd been devoted to for over twenty years. She longed for the safety of Magnolia Shores and the comfort of her family who loved her no matter what. She would return to the Lowcountry as soon as possible.

Grace struggled to focus on her work, but her thoughts kept drifting to Crying Susan. Would her mother forgive her father when she discovered his affair with Claudia? What if Wyatt cheated on Grace? Could she forgive him? Crying Susan's entire life revolved around her husband. At least Kate had her career and a supportive family at Magnolia Shores. All the more reason for Grace to prioritize her professional life. If Wyatt ever left her, she would have her career to fall back on.

Grace pulled out her phone and studied the photos of Claudia and her father. Claudia had perky breasts for someone so old. Grace enlarged the image. Were those even real? She closed out the Photos app and dropped the phone onto her desk.

What good would come from telling her mother? Kate would divorce her father and destroy their family. Maybe Grace could convince her father to break off his relationship with Claudia. The evidence gave Grace the upper hand. She could threaten him. She would tell him if he didn't break up with Claudia, she would . . . *She would what?* she thought, drumming her fingers on her desk.

A thought occurred to Grace, making her sit up straight in her chair. She would blackmail her father. What would she ask for in exchange for her silence? Something for the wedding? The professional fireworks display or getaway helicopter? Better yet, she would ask for money for their kitchen/family room addition.

Grace called her father's cell, and when he didn't answer, she tried his office. His receptionist told Grace he'd gone home early. She checked the time. It was almost five o'clock. Maybe she could catch him at home. She gathered her belongings and left the office.

Grace was disappointed to discover her father wasn't home from work yet. But since her mother was here, she might as well ask Kate about the declined charge for the band deposit. She found her mother in her father's study, sitting in his desk chair and staring out the window at the parched backyard. "Mom? What're you doing in here?"

Kate spun the chair around to face her. She looked awful, her face pale and eyes swollen.

"Have you been crying? What's wrong?" Maybe Kate had found out about the affair on her own. Which was both good and bad. Grace wouldn't have to tell her, but she'd have to wait longer for her new kitchen.

Kate hesitated as though deciding what to say. "You might as well know. You'll eventually find out anyway," she said with a deep sigh as she rose slowly from the chair.

"Find out what?" Grace asked, her skin prickling even though she already knew.

"Your father invested a lot of money in an experimental medical device that didn't pan out."

Grace tensed. This was not at all what she'd expected. "How much money?"

"Our joint savings and then some," Kate said with a grim expression.

Grace's brow shot up. "Are you saying you're broke?"

"We're not destitute. Fortunately, we still have our careers. We'll recover the loss in time."

"In time? But what about my wedding?"

Anger flickered in her mother's hazel eyes. "I don't know,

Grace. This is all such a shock. I'll have to think about it. Maybe I'll use my own savings for a small wedding."

Panic gripped Grace's chest. *A small wedding? This can't be happening.*

Her mother let out a loud sob that echoed throughout the house. Kate was usually calm and collected. Seeing her so upset unnerved Grace. Maybe there was something else wrong. Did she know about her father's affair?

Grace hugged her mom. "Don't cry, Mom. It's just money. Or is it more than that? I hope no one is sick. It's not Izzy, is it?"

Kate shook her head as she pushed Grace away. "Everyone is healthy, which I should be grateful for. I'm not myself right now, and I need to be alone," she said, brushing past Grace on the way out of the room.

Grace bolted out the front door and sped away from the house. Instead of going to Wyatt's parents' guest cottage, she drove straight home. She, too, needed to be alone with her thoughts. She'd promised Wyatt she wouldn't talk about the wedding, but the wedding was all she could think about right now. She was furious with her father. Anyone with a brain knew not to invest all their eggs in one basket.

Removing their bottle of Tito's from the freezer, she filled a shot glass, downed it, and poured herself another. She took the shot glass and the bottle outside to the table on the porch, ignoring Wyatt's texts about meeting him at their favorite ATX-Mex restaurant for dinner. But when he called, she picked up the phone, answering with a gloomy hello.

"Grace! Where are you? I was getting worried about you. Why didn't you respond to my texts?"

Grace massaged her temples. "I'm at home. I'm sorry, Wyatt, but I'm not very good company tonight. Go ahead to dinner without me."

"You don't sound good. Did you break the news about your father's affair to your mom?"

"I didn't get a chance. I went over there, but Mom is dealing with another crisis, and I didn't think she could handle hearing about Dad's affair," Grace explained, twisting the truth. Her fiancé didn't need to know she'd been planning to blackmail her own father.

"What crisis? Did someone die?"

"No, it's nothing like that. I'll explain when I see you tomorrow. I'm going to stay here tonight."

"I'm coming over," Wyatt said, hanging up before she could protest.

Grace drank another shot before returning the vodka to the freezer. Hurrying upstairs to their bathroom, she gargled with mouthwash and pulled her hair back in a ponytail. She was waiting on the front steps when Wyatt pulled up.

"You look like you lost your best friend. What on earth is going on?" he asked, sitting down beside her.

She explained about her father's failed investment and her parents' subsequent financial crisis.

"You scared me. I thought something was really wrong?"

"Something *is* really wrong, Wyatt. My father is a creep. He took my mother's money without asking, and he's cheating on her."

"You're right. Those are big problems, but not insurmountable. Your parents are adults. They'll figure out their lives for themselves. They don't need us interfering."

"Except for the obvious. They can't afford to pay for our wedding. And since you've forbidden me to talk about our wedding, you should leave now so I can be depressed alone," Grace said, getting up and going inside.

He followed her into the kitchen. "I'm not a dictator, Grace, and I didn't *forbid* you to talk about the wedding. I merely asked you to lay off the subject because you were becoming obsessed. We have our savings. We can pay for a small wedding ourselves."

"No way! That's our kitchen money. Parents are supposed to pay for their kid's wedding." A thought suddenly occurred to

Grace. "Mom's family is wealthy. Maybe Izzy can pay for our wedding."

Wyatt's face beamed red. "I refuse to accept handouts from your grandmother. I see nothing wrong with us paying for our wedding. We both have good salaries. It won't take us long to earn the money back."

Grace glared at him. "Just stay out of it, Wyatt. I can handle my parents."

His eyes bore into hers. "You care more about the wedding than the marriage."

She folded her arms over her chest. "That's not true. But think whatever you want. I warned you not to come over here."

Wyatt deflated, his shoulders slumping. "I'm done with this. As far as I'm concerned, the wedding is off."

She glared at him. "You don't mean that."

"Like hell I don't," he said, bolting out of the house.

Grace debated whether to go after him or to retrieve the vodka from the refrigerator. The vodka won.

twenty-two

K ate called the landline at Magnolia Shores and asked Shelby to put Blossom on the phone. Her efforts to sound normal failed. Shelby knew her too well.

"What's wrong, Mom? You sound like you've been crying."

"Nothing, sweetheart. I just need some advice."

Shelby chuckled. "Blossom has plenty of that. Let me find her. I'll have her call you back from my cell phone."

"Thanks, love. Sorry to drag you away from work."

Kate paced around the house, waiting anxiously for Blossom to return her call. Short of breath and hands trembling, she felt on the verge of a panic attack. Her imagination ran wild. The scent of jasmine assaulted her nose, and everywhere she looked, she envisioned her husband and best friend having sex—in her bed, on the family room sofa, in their marble shower.

When her phone finally rang, she went outside to the porch to talk to Blossom.

"What's wrong, Katie girl?" Blossom asked.

Kate managed to tell Blossom about the failed investment and her husband's affair before bursting into tears. "What do I do, Blossom?"

"That's a loaded question. Are you ready to leave him?"

"Yes! He cheated on me with my best friend. I can't think of a worse betrayal."

"I agree. But it's my job to ask. Are you ready to come home?"

The word *home* never sounded so good. This house had been Kate's temporary home for the past thirty years, a dwelling she'd filled with love where she raised her girls. But Magnolia Shores was her real home, where her heart resided. "I should never have left," Kate said in a weak voice.

"Then what're you waiting for? Get on a plane and get yourself back down here."

Kate considered her options. If she flew, she would arrive in Charleston by midnight and wake up in her bed in the cottage at Magnolia Shores tomorrow morning. But this wasn't a visit. She would be staying for good this time. "I should drive. I'll need my car and all my clothes."

"You're in no shape to drive alone. I'll cover for Shelby so she can fly to Texas and ride home with you."

Blossom's suggestion tempted her. She dreaded the eighteen-hour drive alone. But she'd have to wait for Shelby to get here, and she hated for her daughter to take so much time off from work. "I'll be fine by myself. The long drive will give me time to think and clear my head. Should I consult a divorce attorney before I leave?"

"That's up to you. Are you in the right frame of mind to seek legal advice?"

"Not at all. I should wait. I need to make sure I consult the right attorney anyway."

Silence filled the phone as Kate chewed on her thumbnail.

"I sense your hesitation, Kate. What're you thinking?"

How could she explain to Blossom that she felt guilty for not trying harder to make her marriage work? Had she driven her husband into the arms of another woman? If so, he could've picked someone other than her best friend. She inhaled a deep breath, pulling herself to her full height. There was no turning back. Only full steam ahead.

"Nope. I'm good. I'm going to pack up and hit the road. If I hurry, I can get away before Rand comes home from work."

"Should I say anything to Shelby?" Blossom asked.

"No. She should hear this from me. I'll call both girls from the road."

Kate stuffed her clothes, accessories, and shoes into every suitcase, tote, and gym bag she could find. She packed the jewelry case containing the family heirloom pieces her mother had given her for birthdays and Christmases over the years, but she left her diamond engagement ring and wedding band on top of her chest of drawers.

Retrieving two cardboard boxes from the attic, she filled one with the contents of her desk and the other with framed photographs of the girls taken over the years. She would return for the rest of her valuables once the house was sold.

Kate was putting the last suitcase in the trunk of her Volvo wagon when Rand pulled into the driveway and got out of the car. "What're you doing?"

"I'm leaving you." She slammed the rear door and headed back inside for her purse.

He followed her into the kitchen. "But why? Aren't we going to work things out? You agreed to couple's therapy."

She whirled around to face him. "*I* agreed to therapy? I'm the one who has been trying to get *you* to seek counseling for years," she said, jabbing her finger into his chest. "But you've been too busy screwing my best friend."

The color drained from his face. "How'd you find out?"

"How could I *not* find out? You left a trail of evidence a mile long. You reeked of Claudia's new Enchanted Garden perfume when you came home last night. And my robe smells of it too. How dare you let your mistress wear my bathrobe? And I found this in the pocket of your navy sports coat." Kate tugged the tube of lipstick out of her pocket and threw it at him.

He shielded himself from the flying lipstick. "Is that all?"

"Isn't that enough?" Kate planted her hands on her hips.

"Don't try to tell me it was a one-night hookup, that it didn't mean anything, because I read your string of text messages. You two have been sleeping together under my nose for more than two years."

"How did you read those messages?" His eyes narrowed. "Did you log onto my computer?"

"You bet. You really should change your passcode. You're hiding sensitive information. Seriously, Rand, those photographs you and Claudia shared were downright vulgar. Why does it matter how I found out about your affair anyway?"

His gaze fell to the floor. "I thought maybe Grace told you."

Kate's brow hit her hairline. "You mean Grace knows about this?"

Rand nodded. "One day a few weeks ago, she came by the house looking for something wedding related. She ran into Claudia in the kitchen. Grace flew immediately to South Carolina. I was shocked she didn't rat me out."

Kate's mind reeled as she remembered her daughter's sudden appearance. "Why didn't she tell me?"

"Because she feared a divorce would ruin her wedding."

"Well, there won't be a wedding now since you blew all our money on some bogus medical device invention." Kate swung her purse over her shoulder and brushed past him. "Have a nice life, Rand. My attorney will be in touch," she said and fled the house, slamming the front door behind her.

Kate had driven several blocks when she realized Claudia's husband didn't know about the affair. She called Bobby and explained the situation as best she could. To her surprise, Bobby was relieved.

"Good!" he said. "Rand can have her. She's made my life miserable these past few years. Those two deserve each other." His tone softened. "I'm sorry, Kate. This must be hard for you. Claudia was your best friend."

"I still can't believe Claudia would do this to me. Or Rand. I got hit by a double whammy." Kate paused for a long minute. "I'm leaving town, Bobby. I wish you the best of luck."

"Same to you, Kate. You've been a good friend to Claudia. Maybe one day she'll realize what a colossal mistake she made in betraying you."

"I'm not holding my breath," Kate said and hung up.

Thirty minutes outside of town, Kate's phone blew up with texts and calls from Claudia. Kate silenced her phone, and when she stopped for gas, she blocked Claudia's number. Losing her best friend felt like a much greater loss than losing her husband. But Grace, her own daughter, keeping this secret from her felt like the ultimate betrayal. She powered off her phone, avoiding the temptation to give Grace a piece of her mind. She needed to calm down first, or she would undoubtedly say something she would regret.

As Austin grew more distant in her rearview mirror, Kate cycled through her emotions. Her sadness morphed into self-pity, which succumbed to anger. By the time she reached Houston, she was utterly exhausted.

twenty-three

· · ·

"Wow! You look amazing," Josh said when he arrived at Magnolia Shores to pick her up. His appreciative gaze as he took in her slim-fitting yellow sundress told Shelby he meant it. Her hair was blown straight, and she'd added only a touch of mascara and clear lip gloss. Testing him, she had chosen not to cover her freckles with makeup. She couldn't date someone who disapproved of her freckles.

"You look pretty awesome yourself," she said about his dressy khaki shorts and green-striped polo. His dark hair was still damp from the shower, and he smelled fresh, like the morning air after a hard night's rain.

"Where are we going?" she asked as they left the property in his pickup truck.

"I made a reservation at Myrtle's Bed and Breakfast. Tonight is her soft opening. She'll soon be serving dinner several nights a week. She's a fabulous cook. I hope that's okay with you."

"That's perfectly fine. I like trying new places."

"I have a feeling we're in for a real treat," he said. "Her prix fixe menu includes a fried green tomato appetizer, beef tenderloin, and lobster mac and cheese."

"Sounds delicious. And expensive," Shelby added under her breath.

"Myrtle is giving me a discount, as in she's comping our meals. Callie and I have been sprucing up her courtyard garden."

Shelby laughed. "Of course. She's obviously pleased with your work. I can't wait to see the garden. Will Callie be here?" Shelby said, relishing the idea of seeing his super-hip twin.

"Nah. Callie's going to some concert tonight. No surprise there."

Myrtle, a small woman with silver-streaked hair, greeted them at the entrance to her side garden with Champagne cocktails in stemless flutes. "Welcome to my soft opening. Thank you for allowing me to experiment on you," she said with a girlish giggle.

Josh spread his arms wide. "I'm starving. Experiment away."

Myrtle pinched his cheek. "You're such a dear boy." She turned her attention to Shelby. "And who is your lovely date?"

Shelby extended her hand. "I've heard a lot about you, Myrtle, and I'm glad to finally meet you. I'm Shelby Kinder, Isabelle St. Clair's granddaughter."

"So, you're my new competition. I hear things are going well for your bed and breakfast."

"Yes, ma'am. We had a rocky start, but we're working through our challenges."

"I'm glad to hear it. The competition will keep me on my toes. Let me show you to your table."

Every step along the torch-lined cobblestone path felt like a journey into a storybook realm. Fairy lights danced among lush foliage, and summer flowers scented the air. Myrtle guided them to a secluded table for two tucked away at the back of the small outdoor dining area. Nearby, a fountain trickled water, and above them, a pergola draped in blooming pink roses provided a canopy. In the center of the table, light flickered from a fat pillar candle nestled in a hurricane lantern.

"I'm blown away by your garden, Myrtle. It's . . ."—Shelby searched for the right word—"magical."

Myrtle beamed. "Thank you, my dear. The praise belongs to my young landscape crew." She rested a hand on Josh's shoulder. "Our little town is blessed to have talent like Josh's and Callie's."

Shelby waited for Myrtle to leave before congratulating Josh on his garden. "You're making quite a name for yourself," she said, taking in their surroundings. "This is very cutting-edge." When the time came, she would suggest they hire Josh and Callie to design the landscape for The Sanctuary.

As black-and-white-clad servers delivered course after course of the most delicious food Shelby had ever tasted, Josh entertained her with funny stories from his work escapades. His sparkling blue eyes mesmerized her, and she hung on his every word. He was funny, attentive, and boy-next-door normal. She sensed he was steady, someone she could count on, polar opposites of Drama King Matt.

By the time they finished lemon blueberry cheesecake bars for dessert, Shelby was mildly tipsy from two glasses of wine. But not Josh. Because he was driving, he had switched to sweet tea after the Champagne cocktail.

Josh pointed out the full moon as they left Myrtle's. "It's still early. Do you have time to walk along the waterfront? Or do you need to get home?"

"My uncle is covering for me. Our guests are probably back from dinner now anyway. Can we go back to the Mathesons' house? The view of the moon must be incredible from their pool."

"Great idea," he said and headed across the Merriweather Bridge.

When they arrived at the contemporary white house, Josh parked his truck in the driveway. They walked around to the property's waterside, standing at the edge of the pool deck, staring up at the moonlit sky.

"It's so beautiful," Shelby said in awe.

Josh turned to face her. "Not as beautiful as you." He touched the tip of his tongue to her cheek.

She giggled as she stepped back. "What're you doing?"

"Something I've wanted to do all night. I'm tasting your freckles."

"Oh? And what do they taste like?"

"Not sure. I need another lick." Hooking an arm around her waist, he drew her close and dragged his tongue over her cheek. He smacked his lips and said, "Super sweet, like the season's first strawberries."

Shelby gave him a mental check mark for passing the freckle test. "Ha ha. Strawberry like my coloring. Clever."

Cupping her face, he pressed his lips against hers. "You're sweet all over," he said in a husky voice.

While she didn't experience the frenzied burning passion she had with Matt, she found comfort in his arms, as though this was where she belonged. He made her feel wanted, less empty inside, like no one else ever had. After Matt's rejection, she was desperate to regain her sense of worth.

The romantic setting—the moon shimmering off the water and the ocean waves lapping gently against the sand—cast a spell over her, and when Josh lifted her dress over her head, she didn't stop him. He stripped off his clothes, and they stretched out together on a lounge chair. She warned him she wasn't on the pill, and he promised to be careful.

Josh made love to her with a tenderness that brought tears to her eyes and took her to soaring heights. Afterward, he held her in his strong arms. "You're stunning, Shelby. I hope you realize how special you are."

She nestled closer to him. "I think you're pretty special too. I don't sleep around, Josh. I was in a long-term relationship during high school and college. You're only the third guy I've been with."

"You don't have to explain, but I appreciate your honesty. I really like you, Shelby. I realize we've only been out twice, but I'm not interested in anyone else. Would you consider being exclusive with me?"

His question took her by surprise. While she wasn't ready to be exclusive with anyone, Josh was a catch—gorgeous, successful, and trustworthy—and she didn't want him to slip away. Would Matt be jealous when he found out? Why was she thinking about Matt at a time like this? Maybe Josh could help her get Matt out of her head.

"Can we be exclusive without being boyfriend and girlfriend?"

Josh flashed her a pearly white smile. "Sure thing. We can be whatever you want. We won't see other people, but we'll take our time getting to know each other better."

They dressed and returned to the pool's edge for one last look at the moon. "Since we're exclusive, do you mind if I post a selfie of us on Instagram," Shelby asked, holding up her phone.

"Not at all. Here. Let me do it. My arms are longer," he said, taking the phone from her.

Turning away from the water, he snapped a half dozen images of them with the moon in the background. As they walked back to Josh's truck, she posted the best pic on Instagram with the catchy caption—*Under the spell of moonlit magic.* A pang of guilt gripped her chest. Was she using Josh to make Matt jealous?

Shelby was quiet on the short drive back to Magnolia Shores. She'd been careless in having unprotected sex with both Matt and Josh. She had a packet of birth control pills left over from when she was in a relationship with Luke. As soon as her next period ended, she would start taking those and schedule an appointment with a local gynecologist.

twenty-four

· · ·

At one o'clock in the morning, Kate's vision grew blurry from staring at the dark highway, and she checked into a roadside hotel in Mobile, Alabama. She zonked out and slept soundly until nine the following morning. She woke feeling refreshed and ready to face her new life without Rand. Eager to get home to Magnolia Shores, she quickly showered and dressed. After checking out of the hotel, she stopped by Starbucks for a coffee and breakfast sandwich. While waiting in the drive-through line, she checked her phone for the first time since leaving Austin. She had five missed calls and a pleading text message from Grace.

> Mom, please call me. We need to talk about my wedding.

Kate waited until she was on the highway heading toward Montgomery before clicking on Grace's number. Her phone connected to Bluetooth, and ringing filled the car. Grace answered in a groggy hello.

"Grace? Are you okay? You don't sound good."

"I was sleeping."

Kate glanced at the dashboard clock. "It's nearly eleven o'clock. Why aren't you at work? Are you sick?"

"I'm taking a mental health day. Where are you? I've been trying to call you."

"I'm on the way to South Carolina. I'm leaving your father, Grace. He's having an affair with Claudia. But you already know that. Why didn't you tell me?"

"I . . . um . . ." The sound of rustling bed covers filled the line, and when Grace spoke again, she sounded more alert. "Claudia assured me it only happened once. I was trying to protect you. I didn't want to ruin your marriage over a random hookup. I did a little snooping when I got home on Saturday, and I caught Dad and Claudia together again. I was coming over to tell you about it yesterday, but you were so angry at Dad for taking your savings I figured it could wait. But now you know, so I don't have to be the bad guy."

Kate could hardly believe her ears. How could her daughter be so insensitive? Before she could respond, Grace blurted, "Mom, I need to know about my wedding."

Kate gripped the steering wheel. *Is this kid for real? My life has fallen apart, and all she thinks about is herself.* "What about your wedding, Grace?"

"You mentioned using your savings to pay for it. Is that still a possibility?"

Kate yearned to rip her daughter a new one, but she managed to hold her tongue. "I can't think about that right now, Grace."

"But, Mom!" Grace protested in a shrill voice. "This is my entire life we're talking about."

"And this is my entire life too. I'll call you in a few days," Kate said, hanging up on her.

Kate pressed her foot on the accelerator in frustration. She was furious at herself, not only for raising such a self-centered young woman but for even considering passing up a golden business opportunity to pay for Grace's wedding. When she saw a state trooper in the median, she slowed down. A speeding ticket was the last thing she needed right now.

She drove a few more miles until she felt calmer before calling Shelby. Her youngest also sounded blue. "What's wrong, sweetheart?"

"Nothing, really. I'm just tired. You sound like you're in the car. Where are you?"

"I'm in Alabama, heading back to South Carolina. I have bad news, Shelby. Your father and I are splitting up," she said and explained Rand's failed business venture to her youngest.

"What are you saying, Mom? Are y'all broke?"

"I can't speak for your father, but I still have my savings. Unfortunately, there's more bad news. Your father and Claudia are having an affair."

Shelby's gasp filled the car. "What? But Claudia is your best friend."

Kate's chest ached like a knife stabbing her in the heart. "I'm aware."

"Wait a minute," Shelby said. "Does Grace know about this?"

Kate frowned at the question. "Why do you ask that?"

"Because I saw Grace talking to Dad on Saturday when he was here. They were too far away for me to hear what they were saying, but they appeared serious, as though they were conspiring about something. And they mentioned Claudia."

Kate's anger flared again, and she cautioned herself not to get riled up. "None of that matters now, sweetheart. My marriage and friendship are over."

"I'm sad about the circumstances, but selfishly, I'm thrilled you're coming back to Magnolia Shores. Are you planning to stay for good this time?"

"That's the idea." Kate looked in the rearview mirror at the suitcases piled high in the back of her car. "I brought all my clothes with me."

"What time do you think you'll get in?"

Kate counted the hours on her fingers. "Sometime early evening."

"Cool! We'll have dinner together."

"That would be great. But please don't go to any trouble. We'll eat whatever we can find in the kitchen. One more thing before we hang up," Kate said in a tone more serious. "Your father and I were married for thirty years. I hope we can one day be friends. The last thing I want is to come between you two."

"No worries, Mom. I already told you Dad and I haven't been close in years. Besides, I feel like he betrayed me too. Cheating on you is like cheating on me."

"Thank you for your support, sweetheart. I needed to hear that right now. I'll see you soon."

Rand's relationship with his daughters was no longer her concern. From now on, she would answer to no one but herself. She'd completed the difficult task of breaking the news to her girls, and hoped the rest would be uphill from here. She would take a few days to let her new reality sink in before she made any drastic decisions about Grace's wedding and her business venture.

Matt arrived with the survey crew around three on Tuesday afternoon. He supervised them as they measured and photographed the future construction site. When they finished, he stuck his head inside the door to tell Shelby he was leaving. When he saw her alone at her desk, he entered the living room.

"I read your post. Are you and Josh exclusive now?"

She flashed him her brightest smile. "We are!"

"You certainly didn't waste any time?"

Her smile faded. "What do you mean?"

"You and I had something special. And the minute I go on a

date with someone else, you jump into a relationship with the first guy who comes along."

Shelby shot out of her chair. "How dare you say that to me? You're the one who has been jerking me around. You came over here on Saturday night, declaring your feelings for me, and the next day, you acted like nothing happened."

"I told you I don't remember what I said that night."

"In that case, I'll remind you. You called me a smoke show. You said you wanted to be with me no matter my age. That I'm inside your head, and you think about me all the time."

"Do you blame me after you had sex with me in the boat? That was hot. What guy wouldn't like that?"

With a huff, she folded her arms over her chest. "If you truly feel that way, why are you with Ada?"

Matt leveled his gaze on her. "Because Ada is mature. She knows what she wants in life. And she doesn't play games."

"You're the one playing games. Ugh! You're the most infuriating person I've ever met, Matt Hitchcock."

Blossom appeared in the doorway. "I heard you two in the kitchen. Is everything all right in here?"

"Everything is fine. Matt was just leaving." Coming around the desk, Shelby grabbed Matt's arm and marched him out the front door.

"We're going to be working together, Matt. If we can't figure out how to get along, I'll have to ask Will to make someone else the project manager."

He glared at her. "You wouldn't."

"I would. You care about your job as much as I care about mine. Stay out of my way, and we won't have a problem. Coincidentally, I do know what I want out of life. I want a guy who's attentive, respectful, and concerned about my feelings."

Matt rolled his eyes. "Let me guess. Josh is that someone."

"At least he doesn't jerk me around like you." Shelby spun on her heels and went back inside.

She leaned against the closed door, her heart pounding and tears threatening. Her efforts to convince herself she didn't have feelings for him were not working.

Shelby returned to her desk, but thoughts of Matt prevented her from focusing on her work. She never knew guys could be so fickle, but his constantly changing feelings for her were giving her whiplash.

Around five thirty, she went to help Blossom in the kitchen. When Shelby informed Blossom of her mother's homecoming earlier in the day, they'd invited Pritchard for dinner and planned a simple meal of homemade pizza and salad.

Shelby slid onto the counter and watched silently as Blossom made the pizza sauce at the stove.

Blossom glanced up at her. "You're awfully quiet, baby girl. Something's eating at you. Was it your argument with Matt earlier?"

"That was part of it." Shelby sighed. "I'm so confused, Blossom. I have feelings for both Matt and Josh. Matt makes me crazy, and Josh is a super nice guy. I'm not one to sleep around. Before I came here, I'd only been with one guy."

"Luke?" Blossom asked, and Shelby nodded.

Shelby swiped angrily at the tear on her cheek. "I had sex with both Matt and Josh in the same week. I guess that makes me a slut."

"Not necessarily." Blossom removed the pot from the eye and turned off the stove. "How did these incidents happen? Were they spur of the moment? Had you been drinking?"

"Yes, and yes. Matt happened to stop by after my awful argument with Grace, and I literally threw myself at him. I was so upset and needed to release all the pent-up anger. It was the middle of the day, and I had not been drinking."

Blossom moved closer to her. "But you had with Josh?"

"I had a couple of glasses of wine at dinner, but I wasn't drunk, and I knew what I was doing. He's so caring and gentle. He makes me feel special, and I wanted to be with him." Shelby could no longer hold back the tears. "I don't know what's wrong with me, Blossom. I should be happy. My career is going well. I love living in the Lowcountry. I'm meeting lots of new people. But I feel so empty inside. Maybe I was looking to Matt and Josh to fill me up."

"Sounds like a plausible explanation to me." Blossom tore a paper towel off the roll and handed it to her to wipe her tears. "But it didn't work, did it?"

"No!" Shelby sobbed into her balled fist.

Blossom touched the tip of her finger to Shelby's chin. "Because only you can fill the void."

"How do I do that?"

"First, you have to determine what's missing." Blossom squeezed her thigh. "Don't be too hard on yourself, baby girl. Your life has been a whirlwind these past couple of months. You are probably just reacting to all the changes."

"Do you really think so?" Shelby asked, blowing her nose into the paper towel.

"It's possible. Or there could be a more deep-seated problem you need to address. But you're doing the right thing by talking about it. Maybe try distancing yourself from both fellas until you feel more like yourself."

"I'll try, but it's hard. I enjoy hanging out with them. Josh, anyway. Matt has become a real pill."

Blossom chuckled. "You're a lovely young woman with much to offer the world. There will always be handsome young men interested in you. But you can't make someone else happy until you've made yourself happy."

"That makes sense." Shelby slid off the counter to her feet and fell into Blossom's arms. "Thank you for listening."

"Anytime, baby girl." Blossom whispered to her, "Do I need to ask if you used protection?"

Shelby shook her head as she pulled away from Blossom. "And I'm not on the pill. Everything happened so fast with Matt, I didn't give him a chance to use a condom, and Josh didn't have one on him. I wasn't worried about it at the time with either of them. But now, I'm freaking out. What if I'm pregnant?"

"Then you'll deal with it. You can't turn back the clock." Blossom cupped Shelby's cheek. "You must take life as it comes, Shelby. You're blessed to have wonderful people who care very much about you. Whatever happens, you are not alone."

twenty-five

. . .

Despite having asked Shelby not to go to any trouble for her homecoming, Kate was grateful to see her family waiting in the courtyard at Magnolia Shores upon her arrival. Pritchard opened her car door and helped her out.

"My stiff muscles thank you," Kate said, stretching. "I'm surprised to see you. I thought you'd be in Nashville."

Pritchard chuckled. "I keep postponing my departure. I used a meeting with Will as my first excuse. And your homecoming has given me a reason to stay. I'll eventually have to go and move out of my apartment, but I'm trying to wrap up most loose ends virtually."

Kate threw her arms around her brother. "Well, I'm eternally grateful. I didn't realize how much I need my family right now."

"We're here for you, sis," he whispered.

Turning away from her brother, she drew Blossom and Shelby in for a group hug. "You two are a sight for sore eyes. I've only been gone for two days, but it feels like an eternity."

"I'm just glad you're back safely," Shelby said.

"Magnolia Shores wasn't the same without you," Blossom added.

Kate embraced her mother last. "I hope you don't mind having a roommate again."

"I don't mind a bit. I'm sorry for your troubles, darling girl. But I'm overjoyed to have you back home, where you belong," Izzy said, her speech improved, nearly back to normal.

"You sound like your old self again."

"I'm beginning to feel like my old self. I hope you don't think all of that will fit in there," Izzy said, gesturing with her cane at the luggage in Kate's car and then at the cottage.

Kate laughed. "Not at all. I'll store most of it in the attic until we move back into the main house after Labor Day. Does anyone want to help me unpack?" she asked with a sheepish grin.

"Unpacking can wait," Pritchard said. "Let's eat first, and we'll all help you after dinner."

Kate felt the tension drain from her body. Returning home to her family was the right move. "That works for me." Her gaze shifted to Blossom. "But I hope you didn't go to any trouble."

Blossom shook her head, the yellow hibiscus flower bobbing up and down in her hair. "Not a bit. We're having homemade pizza and salad."

Kate's stomach rumbled. She hadn't eaten anything since her Starbucks breakfast sandwich. "Pizza sounds delicious."

"I have a drink waiting for you in the kitchen," Shelby said, looping her arm through Kate's.

"I could use one after the long drive," Kate said, and they migrated across the courtyard to the kitchen.

Shelby handed her a clear, fizzy beverage in a lowball glass.

Kate sipped the drink. "Delicious and refreshing. What's it called?" she asked, assuming it was one of Shelby's concoctions.

"A vodka soda," Shelby said, and everyone laughed.

A celebratory mood settled over the small group as they ate. Kate and Pritchard entertained the others with tales from their youth. Even Izzy had never heard about some of their mischievous escapades.

After dinner, Blossom and Izzy tackled the dishes while Pritchard, Shelby, and Kate unpacked her car.

When Shelby returned to the main house to check on their guests, Pritchard told Kate, "I brought my bathing suit with me. Can I interest you in a swim?"

Kate's face lit up. "Yes! I would love that. I'll change and meet you at the pool in ten minutes."

Locating her bathing suit in her mountain of luggage took much longer. When Kate arrived, Pritchard was floating on a raft in the pool.

She grabbed a second raft from the shed and dove into the pool. "The water feels amazing. Just what the doctor ordered for my stiff muscles."

"Mm-hmm. It's a gorgeous night." Pritchard closed his eyes, folding his hands on his chest. "And so peaceful."

They floated for a while, not talking but listening to the crickets chirping and the tree frogs singing.

Finally, Kate broke their silence. "I made the right decision to come home. Mom is right. I belong here. As Blossom says, home is the anchor of our soul, and my anchor is sunk in deep."

Pritchard rolled his head to look at her. "I feel the same way about retiring and leaving Nashville. Water's Edge is my happy place."

"Isn't it hard with Savannah working nights? Don't you miss having her around?"

"Very much. But once we open The Sanctuary next summer, we'll be together all the time."

Realizing that Kate would now be a part of opening The Sanctuary boosted her spirits.

"So, what's next for you now that you're back?" Pritchard asked. "Will you start developing your lighting business right away?"

"Lumina Designs may have to wait. I may use my savings for Grace's wedding."

Ashley Farley

Pritchard lifted his head off the raft. "How much savings are we talking about?"

"Nearly two hundred thousand."

His blue eyes bugged out. "Whoa, Kate. That's a lot of money to spend on a wedding. Our budget for Harper's wedding is a third of that. And we're not cutting any corners."

"I'm aware. My eldest has extravagant tastes, and this wedding means the world to her. She's dreamed of this day her entire life. As a child, she insisted I bring her a slice of cake every time I attended a wedding. She'd wait up for me to come home to hear about the reception."

"All little girls dream of their wedding days, Kate. Thanks to your derelict husband, your family is in a financial crisis. While it's not my place to say this, considering the circumstances, she should downscale her dream wedding."

"You're my brother, Pritchard. You can say anything you'd like to me. But even a scaled-down wedding won't leave me enough for my business venture."

"You're not being fair to yourself, Kate. We're talking about your future, your career. You've worked hard to save that money. Blowing it on a grandiose wedding seems irresponsible."

"I agree with you, but I can't deny my daughter her big day."

"So instead, you're denying yourself your golden career opportunity?"

"I guess so." Kate rolled off her raft and into the water. She swam under her brother's float and tipped him over, playfully dunking him until his arms flailed, and he gasped for air. When she set him free, they flung themselves belly-down onto the same raft.

"You could always borrow money from Dad's estate," Pritchard suggested.

"I wouldn't feel right doing that, especially when we're getting ready to expand. If I don't pursue the lighting venture, would you consider giving me a role at the new resort?"

"Not just any role. Magnolia Shores belongs to both of us. I'd love for us to co-manage the resort together."

"Do you think there's enough growth opportunity for both of us?"

"More than enough. Honestly, I'm worried about how I'll manage it alone."

Kate rested her head on her arm. "I admit the prospect of working with you appeals to me."

He tugged a hank of her wet hair. "You've had a rough couple of days. Give yourself time to settle in before you make rash decisions."

twenty-six

. . .

Shelby didn't intentionally eavesdrop on her mother's conversation with Pritchard. She was watering a wilting container plant on the terrace when their voices wafted toward her. The mention of her sister got her attention, and she moved closer to the pool, hiding behind a palmetto tree. She could hardly believe her ears. Her mother was considering spending the two hundred thousand dollars she'd saved to start her own lighting company on Grace's wedding. Was she out of her mind?

Shelby's heart pounded as she slipped back inside. She couldn't let her mother make such an enormous sacrifice. She went down to the dock for privacy to call her sister. Her first three attempts went straight to voicemail. She left a message on the fourth. "You can ignore me all you want, Grace, but I won't stop trying until you answer."

Shelby tried one last time for good measure, and her sister answered with a slurred hello.

"Grace! It's about time! Why didn't you answer my calls? Have you been drinking?"

"Not enough. What do you want, Shelby?"

Pacing in circles, Shelby said, "I overheard Mom talking to

Pritchard. Did you know she's been saving money to start her own lighting business?"

Grace snorted. "That's a joke. Mom doesn't know the first thing about running her own business."

Shelby gripped the phone. "Yes, she does," she said in a defensive tone. "She's been working in the industry for more than twenty years. That's not up to you to decide anyway. It's *Mom's* money. You can't let her blow it on *your* wedding."

"Stay out of it, Shelby. I'm her daughter, and she owes me a wedding."

Shelby's anger spiraled. If Grace were here right now, she would punch her in the face. "Listen to yourself, you spoiled brat. Mom owes you nothing. You're making plenty of money. Why don't you pay for your own wedding?"

"Not that it's any of your business, but Wyatt and I are saving to redo our kitchen and expand our house. It's not my fault Dad's investment went bust. It's fine with me if she wants to pay for the wedding."

Shelby stomped the dock in frustration. "Ugh. You're an awful person, Grace."

"Chill, Shelby. Why are you so bent out of shape?" Grace hesitated. "Are you upset your mommy and daddy are getting a divorce? Grow up, little sister."

"You're the one who needs to grow up. Why didn't you tell Mom about Dad's affair with Claudia? There must have been something in it for you to keep a secret that huge."

"I was trying to save our family. Duh."

"Give me a break, Grace. You aren't that noble. Never mind. I don't want to hear your sorry excuses. I'm ashamed to call you my sister," she said, ending the call.

Dropping to the dock, Shelby lay flat on her back, inhaling and exhaling until her breath steadied. She placed her phone on her belly and stared at the night sky. The moon wasn't as full as last night, but it was gorgeous, nonetheless. Why did she let Grace get under her skin? Her volatile relationship with her older sister had always been a source of anxiety and despair for Shelby. Relationships only worked when both parties were committed, and since Grace was clearly not interested in being close, Shelby would have as little interaction with her as possible. Which should be easy with Grace living twelve hundred miles away in Texas. From now on, she would only focus on the positive things in her life. As Blossom said, *You can't make someone else happy until you've made yourself happy.*

Her phone vibrated her belly with an incoming call from Josh. "Hey, Shelby. What're you up to?"

His gentle voice enveloped her in warmth. "I'm on the dock, looking at the moon. What're you doing?"

"I'm craving ice cream. Wanna go to town with me for gelato?"

Shelby hesitated. What if he wanted to have sex again? "It's kinda late."

"It's only nine o'clock. I'm over at my parents' house. We can go by boat. I'll have you home by ten. Do you want me to look like a loser going to Velvet Spoon alone? Puh-lease," he said, sounding like a little boy.

Why not go with him? If he tried to have sex, she would ask him to slow things down. If he really cared about her, he'd understand. "Okay. But only if you're buying. My wallet is up at the house, and I'm too lazy to get it."

"Deal. See you in a few minutes."

Her heart pitter-pattered in anticipation of seeing him again. Her feelings for him were like the gentle breeze blowing off the sound, tender and comforting, wrapping around her heart like a warm embrace.

When he pulled up at the dock ten minutes later, she stepped into the boat and slid onto the seat beside him.

As he navigated away from the dock, he asked, "Are you okay? You look sad."

She shrugged. "I had a fight with my sister."

He leaned into her. "I'm a good listener if you want to talk about it."

Shelby sensed he was a *very* good listener, but she wasn't in the mood for talking. "Another time, maybe. My family's going through some stuff, but my brain hurts from thinking about it." She forced a smile. "What's your favorite gelato flavor?"

He tapped his chin. "That's a hard one. I like so many."

For the rest of the short ride, they discussed their flavor options. When they arrived at the boardwalk, he held her hand as they walked two blocks to the Velvet Spoon. Shelby immediately ordered a single scoop of blackberry lemon basil, while Josh scrutinized the display case for a few minutes before finally settling on cookies and cream.

They walked back to the boardwalk in silence, enjoying their treats.

When Shelby dropped her empty cup in a nearby trash can, Josh said, "Geez! Are you finished already? What a piglet."

"*Piglet*? I only got one scoop." Giggling, she gave him a playful shrug.

"If you weren't turning into a pumpkin at ten, we could go back for more."

Shelby rubbed her belly. "I don't need anymore. That hit the spot. Thank you."

"Thank *you* for coming with me. You saved me from being a lonely loser."

Shelby laughed. She found his goofy personality endearing. "You could never be a loser."

Josh drove slowly away from the dock. When they reached the middle of the sound, he put the boat in neutral and turned toward her, kissing her lightly on the lips. "Yummy. You taste like blackberries and lemons."

She pushed him away. "We need to talk about last night?"

He appeared wounded. "Uh-oh. That doesn't sound good. Are you having regrets?"

She shook her head. "No regrets. Being with you was amazing, but it was a little too soon. It's not your fault. I should have made you stop. Do you mind if we wait until we know each other before it happens again?"

He gave her a warm smile. "I'm totally fine with that. You're in charge. We won't do anything until you give me the green light."

She palmed his cheek. "Thank you for understanding."

"Of course. I really like you, Shelby. I would never do anything to hurt you," he said in a genuine voice that told Shelby he meant it.

Josh was such a good guy. Everything about being with him felt so right. If only her thoughts of Matt would stop intruding . . .

———

Grace had a terrifying thought as she poured the last of the wine into her glass and tossed the bottle into the kitchen trash can. What if Shelby tried to convince Kate to move forward with her lighting venture instead of paying for Grace's wedding?

Turning her phone over, she tapped the screen and accessed her text messages. She read through her stream of unanswered texts to Wyatt, begging him to call her so they could talk. She sounded desperate, like a total loser. She hated giving him the upper hand. And why hadn't he responded? Had he meant what he said yesterday about calling the wedding off? He'd made idle threats before but never acted on them. They'd been together forever. He wouldn't break up with her because he disapproved of her big wedding, would he?

Clicking on Wyatt's location, she was alarmed to see he was at a bar. On a Tuesday night? Who was he with? Was he flirting with girls? Was he already looking to replace Grace?

She yelled at her phone, "Good luck with that, Wyatt. You're not as great as you think you are." Truth be told, Wyatt was her better half, a total catch. The minute word got out about their breakup, he would have girls crawling all over him.

Draining her wine, she considered opening another bottle but decided against it. She could not afford to play hooky from work again. Stumbling to her room, she changed into her nightgown and went into the adjoining bathroom. She brushed her teeth, washed her face, and applied her nightly skin-care regimen.

Studying her reflection in the mirror, she said, "Chin up, Grace! You're a rock star—high school valedictorian, sorority president, magna cum laude graduate. And you're at the top of your professional game as an artificial intelligence engineer. You always land on your feet, and this time will be no different."

She got into bed with her phone and rechecked Wyatt's location. He'd moved to a different bar down the road. She tossed the phone to his side of the bed. "Whatever. I hope you're having fun while I'm alone and miserable here."

She sat straight up in bed. "Wait a minute. I'm going about this all wrong." She should be playing hard to get instead of sending him pathetic text messages. She wouldn't contact him again. She would let him come to her. If he wanted to play chicken, she would not be the one to back down. She realized it was a gamble, and her plan might backfire. But it was the only way she could save face and still get the wedding of her dreams.

As for her mother, she would give Kate a few days to come to terms with her new reality. If she hadn't heard from Kate by Friday, she would pressure her to decide about the wedding.

twenty-seven

. . .

Kate put on a bright face despite the tumult of emotions churning inside her. Despite being exhausted from the long car trip, she slept little on Tuesday night and rose early on Wednesday to prepare breakfast for the guests. After cleanup, she took her mother to physical therapy and lunch afterward at the Custom Crust. She spent the afternoon unpacking and settling into her small room in the cottage. It wasn't until the early evening, as she strolled on the beach toward the Sandy Island Club, that her new reality finally sank in. While she was overjoyed to be permanently back at Magnolia Shores, she was mourning the loss of two very important people in her life. She should be angry at Rand and Claudia. Instead, she felt deep sorrow. Memories from the happy times she spent with both played on a constant reel in her mind throughout the evening, leading to a restless night's sleep.

Kate was squeezing oranges for juice on Thursday morning when a call from Claudia's landline flashed on her phone's screen. When she blocked Claudia's cell number, she'd neglected to block her landline as well. Kate switched her phone to silent, leaving it screen-side-up on the island.

Blossom entered the kitchen a few minutes later. She was

opening a can of dog food when she pointed at Kate's phone. "I'm not being nosy, but I couldn't help but notice you have thirteen missed calls from Claudia. Make that fourteen. I understand why you're avoiding her, but it might be an emergency."

"I hadn't thought of that. I hope nothing has happened to Grace. I guess I have to talk to her," she sighed, wiping her hands on her apron. "Do you mind covering for me? I should only be a minute."

"Not at all. Take your time."

Pouring a cup of coffee, Kate went outside to a table by the pool and waited for Claudia to call again. When her number appeared on the screen, she answered abruptly, "What do you want, Claudia?"

"Geez, Kate. I've been trying to reach you. Why haven't you returned my texts?"

"I blocked your number, and once I know nothing is wrong, I'm going to block this one as well."

"But something is wrong!" Claudia said in a shrill voice. "I'm worried sick about Rand. He's distraught over not being able to afford Grace's wedding. Since you have the money, you should pay for it."

Kate shot to her feet like a spring uncoiling, spilling coffee down the front of her apron. "You have some nerve! How dare you call me with concern about *my* husband. Who pays for our daughter's wedding is none of your business."

"I'm Grace's godmother and Rand's new live-in girlfriend, which makes it my business."

Kate's blood boiled. "Are you kidding me, right now? I've been gone for two days, and you've already moved into *my* house."

"Emotionally, you've been gone for years, Kate."

Claudia's comment cut Kate like a knife. *For years,* her best friend had been sleeping with her husband. Had they been making fun of her behind her back all that time? All those nights

Kate had waited for Rand to come home for dinner, had he been with Claudia?

A lightbulb went off in Kate's rattled mind. As the mother of two sons, Claudia often lamented missing the opportunity to be the mother of the bride. "Wait a minute. I see what this is about. Grace's wedding is your opportunity to take center stage as the father of the bride's significant other." She dumped her coffee out in a nearby bush. "Did my cowardly husband put you up to calling me?"

"I . . . um . . . No, I *offered* to call you since he's so busy at the hospital."

"Don't let him fool you, Claudia. He's not that busy. And by the way, he took out a home equity loan on the house to invest more money in his medical device. Did he mention he's completely broke?"

Claudia's silence told Kate that she was unaware of the extent of Rand's financial trouble.

"You two deserve each other," Kate said and hung up on her.

She blocked Claudia's number, pocketed her phone, and returned to the kitchen. As she picked up the knife to slice open a cantaloupe, tears sprung to Kate's eyes.

"How'd it go?" Blossom asked, returning from chatting with the guests in the dining room.

Kate sniffled as she blotted away her tears with the back of her hand. "Not good," she mumbled.

As she stared down at the floor, Blossom's pink high-top sneakers entered her line of vision. "Uh-oh. Wanna talk about it?"

Looking up at Blossom, she noticed Shelby coming down the hall toward the kitchen. She wouldn't be the one to tell her daughter that Rand and Claudia were living together. She wasn't protecting her husband. She was protecting Shelby. Her pleading hazel eyes sought out Blossom's emerald ones. "I can't be here right now. Can you finish with breakfast? Shelby's here. She can help."

Concern etched Blossom's caramel face. "Of course, love bug. But where are you going?"

"I'm not sure. I just need to be alone," Kate said, brushing past Blossom and slipping out the back door.

Kate retrieved her purse from the cottage and made it to her car before bursting into a torrent of tears. She left Sandy Island, crossed over the Merriweather Bridge, and got on the highway heading north. Her sobs filled the car as she drove. She was barely aware of taking the Beaufort exit until she found herself parked in front of Beaufort Abode.

She glanced down at the clock. Five minutes before ten. Ethan should be opening the shop soon. She prayed he hadn't found another partner with whom to pursue his lighting career.

At ten o'clock sharp, Ethan appeared at the door. Spotting her, he squinted to get a closer look. She wiggled her fingers at him as she slid down in her seat. Unlocking the door, he walked across the sidewalk and tapped on her window. "What's up, Kate? Is something wrong? Why are you here so early?"

To her horror, she burst into tears again.

He opened her car door. "Someone needs a friend. Get yourself inside. I'll make you some coffee."

She shook her head. "I can't. I don't want anyone to see me like this."

"I'm here alone. My partner is doing an installation, and clients never come in before eleven, the lazy hoes."

Kate laughed through her tears. "All right," she said reluctantly. "I could use some coffee."

Inside the shop, he instructed her to have a seat at their worktable and disappeared into the back. He returned with two mugs of coffee, and she poured out the sad story of her husband's affair, their financial trouble, and her dilemma about paying for Grace's wedding.

When she finished, Ethan said, "When you said you had to sort out your life, I had no idea you were dealing with so many issues. I don't have children, so I won't pretend to know what you're going through. But I do love a good party. I've planned countless over-the-top weddings during my career. And it always boggles my mind how much money some folks are willing to spend. I mean, seriously. Why not buy a house?"

"Or start a business," Kate said more to herself than Ethan.

"Exactly. You've been hit by two major tsunamis this week. Give yourself some time, Grace. I'll be here if you decide to pursue our business venture."

"Finding you was a stroke of luck. I want this business venture more than anything. If only my relationship with my daughter weren't at stake."

"I'm overstepping here, but your daughter should be angry at her father, not you." He set down his mug and reached across the table for her hand. "I realize we don't know each other very well, but I have a good feeling about you, and there's no one else I trust to be my partner."

"Thank you for your kindness, Ethan. Those were just the words I needed to hear." Kate stood to go. "One way or another, I'll be back in touch soon. I promise not to keep you waiting indefinitely."

Ethan walked her to the door and kissed her cheek. "Consider me a friend, Kate. You can call me anytime about anything."

The burden of her decision weighed heavily on Kate during the drive back to Water's Edge. The luxury of time was against her. The band deposit was due, and the invitations needed to be ordered. So many details required her attention. Her heart wasn't in it. But how did one deny her daughter a wedding?

twenty-eight

· · ·

S helby went to the kitchen window, watching her mother's car speed away. "What's up with Mom? She left without even saying good morning," she said to Blossom, her eyes still on the dusty driveway.

"She's upset. That Claudia woman called her. I'm not sure what they talked about though."

"Claudia should jump in the ocean in front of a school of sharks," Shelby grumbled.

Blossom chuckled. "Shark bait! I love it."

Shelby smiled. "Poor Mom. She is so down. She's trying to be brave, but I can tell she's suffering. I hate my dad for what he did to her."

"*Hate* is a strong word, Shelby. You're upset with your father right now. And understandably so. You just need to adjust to your family's new dynamics."

"I guess," Shelby said, turning away from the window.

"Mark my word, you'll eventually forgive him. Now come help me get this breakfast out for your guests," she said, gesturing at the platters of food on the counter.

"Yes, ma'am," Shelby said, grabbing a tray and delivering it to the buffet in the dining room.

Two hours later, once the guests had been served and the kitchen cleaned, Shelby and Blossom sat down at the table with a plate of leftover pastries and coffee.

"What's this?" Shelby asked, reaching for a sketch pad someone had left on the table.

"I'm not sure, but I think that belongs to your mother," Blossom said, biting into a cream cheese Danish.

Shelby opened the sketch pad and thumbed through the detailed drawings of light fixtures. "These are really good. I didn't know Mom was so talented."

Blossom leaned across the table to better see the drawings. "Good gracious. One doesn't have to be a lighting expert to realize these are spectacular."

"I heard Mom and Pritchard talking the other night. She's been saving her money to start her own lighting company. But now that Dad bankrupted us, she's considering using her savings for Grace's wedding."

Blossom stopped chewing. "Good gracious. No wonder Kate seems so conflicted. That's a difficult decision for a mother to have to make."

"Not when one of your daughters is Grace. My sister doesn't deserve to have Mom pay for her wedding." Shelby recounted her phone conversation with her sister. "Should I tell Mom what Grace thinks? That Mom's idea to start her own business is a joke?"

"I don't know, baby girl. Your mama is already hurting enough. She doesn't need another blow to her self-confidence right now."

Shelby flipped through the drawings again. "Look at these designs. She's probably been working on them for years. We have to do something, Blossom! We can't let her blow all her savings on Grace's wedding."

Blossom arched an eyebrow. "What did you have in mind?"

"I don't know. Something." Closing the sketchbook, Shelby stood up and moved over to the window, twirling a lock of hair as she stared out at the courtyard. "We should have an intervention like people do when they're trying to get their loved ones to stop drinking."

Kate's car appeared in the driveway. Shelby watched her mother park in front of the cottage and head toward the main house. "Here she comes now." She spun around to face Blossom. "Are you with me?"

"I'm sorry, baby girl, but you're on your own. I'll support you. But I will not coerce your mama into making a decision about anything. Only she knows what's best for her."

Shelby plopped back down in the chair. "You're right. Maybe I'll wait. I need more time to think about what to say."

Kate came through the back door, looking as dejected as Shelby had ever seen her. She'd never hated her father more than she did at that moment. "Are you okay, Mom? Where have you been?"

Kate sat down with them at the table. "I drove over to Beaufort to visit a man I'm considering going into business with."

Shelby moved to the edge of her chair. "Really? That's super exciting, Mama. I was watering plants the other night on the terrace and overheard you discussing a career opportunity with Pritchard. Are you starting your own lighting company?"

Anguish filled Kate's face. "I'm considering it. But the situation is complicated."

Shelby nodded at the sketchbook. "I hope you don't mind, but I looked at your designs. They're incredible."

"Thank you, sweetheart. I've been dreaming about and saving for this venture for years. A friend in the industry introduced me to Ethan, the man in Beaufort. He's incredibly talented. He learned his skills from his grandfather. With everything that has happened with your father, I may use my savings to pay for Grace's wedding."

"Never mind she didn't ask her only sister to be a bridesmaid," Shelby mumbled under her breath. If her mother heard her, she didn't react.

Shelby searched Blossom's face for encouragement or a clue about how to proceed. But her expression was blank. Some help she was. Shelby longed to throw her sister under the bus, but instead of hurting Grace, she would hurt her mother.

"Do you have to use all the money for the business? I don't know how much weddings cost, but what if you only used half for the business and the other half for the wedding?" Shelby suggested.

"Grace would have to scale down her wedding," Kate said.

"So? She's not royalty. She should be grateful for whatever wedding you give her."

Kate grimaced. "Unfortunately, I don't think she'll see it that way."

"You could at least talk to her about it. She might surprise you, especially considering what Dad is putting you through." Shelby gave herself a mental high five. She put the ball in Grace's court. However she chose to play it was up to her.

"I'll think about it." Kate stroked Shelby's arm. "I appreciate your concern, sweetheart. But I don't want you worrying about my problems."

"We're a family, Mama. That's what we do." Shelby pushed back from the table. "I need to get to work."

Shelby spent the early afternoon at her desk, organizing room assignments for the coming weekend. Around three o'clock, Josh called about her dinner plans.

Shelby sighed. "You might as well know, Josh. My parents are getting a divorce. My father cheated on my mom with her best friend. Mom's in a funk, and I don't want to leave her." A thought occurred to Shelby. "Why don't you come here? We can cook something on the grill."

"That sounds great! I can help cheer up your mom," he said genuinely. Most guys would run from such an invitation. Josh was proving to be a unicorn.

"I should warn you that my grandmother and a close family friend might join us. I hope you don't mind eccentric old ladies."

"Ha. You just described most of my clients."

They talked for a minute about logistics before hanging up.

When Shelby told her mother about dinner, Kate tried to beg off. "Oh, honey. You don't need Debbie Downer ruining your evening. I'll meet your friend another time."

Shelby pressed her hands together under her chin. "Please, Mama. I'm curious what you think about Josh."

"All right, then. I look forward to meeting him," Kate said with a sad smile.

Josh showed up promptly at seven with a bag of sweet potatoes, a bouquet of zinnias, and a bottle of Symphony wine from Deep Water Vineyard. He handed the zinnias to Kate. "For you."

Kate flashed him a smile. "How thoughtful. They're gorgeous."

Josh beamed. "Thanks! My sister grows flowers for wholesale florists."

Kate's face lit up. "How interesting."

"Josh's family owns Roots and Blooms Garden Center," Shelby explained to her mom. "Are you familiar with it?"

"Yes! Of course! It's been around forever."

Josh nodded. "My grandparents started it back in the sixties. It's come a long way since then."

"Let me get something to put these in." Kate located a vase in the butler's pantry, filled it with water, and arranged the flowers.

They set to work preparing dinner. Josh washed the sweet potatoes, Kate made the salad, and Shelby shucked the corn.

"So, Mom," Shelby said as she cut the kernels off the cob. "Josh and his sister started their own business. Callie designs landscapes, and Josh's lawn care company installs the plant material."

Kate's eyes widened. "Good for you. That's a major accomplishment for someone so young. Do you get along well with your sister?"

"She's my twin, and we get along remarkably well considering our very different personalities," Josh said, slicing the sweet potatoes into wedges. "Our business is tied to the garden center. We've dreamed of expanding our services since we were kids. I guess we inherited the entrepreneurial gene from our grandparents. I can't imagine working for someone else. I love being the captain of my own ship."

Shelby watched her mother hanging on to Josh's every word. The conversation was unfolding just as she'd hoped.

When Josh went outside to start the grill, Kate nudged Shelby. "He's adorable, Shelby. And so accomplished for someone so young."

"Josh works hard. When the time comes, I'm going to suggest Pritchard hire Josh and Callie to design the gardens for The Sanctuary."

"That's a great idea! Have you seen any of their work?" Kate asked, rinsing a handful of grape tomatoes and adding them to her salad.

"Yes! They turned Myrtle's backyard into an enchanted garden. Josh took me there for dinner the other night. You should stop by sometime and check it out. It's truly amazing."

"I will. I didn't realize Myrtle had started serving dinner."

Shelby bobbed her head. "We attended the soft opening. She's a fabulous cook."

Josh returned, announcing the grill was ready for the burgers. He opened the chilled wine and poured three glasses.

Kate took a sip. "This is delicious. I taste both floral and citrus notes." She examined the bottle. "I've never heard of Deep Water Vineyard. Where is it located?"

"On Wadmalaw Island. They grow muscadine grapes, but surprisingly, their wines aren't overly sweet as you might expect."

Shelby removed the platter of burgers from the refrigerator. "Here! If you take these, I'll bring the stuff to set the table." She handed him the burgers and gathered the placemats, napkins, and utensils she'd set out on the counter earlier.

When the burgers were done, Blossom and Izzy joined them at

the table on the terrace. As they ate, Josh charmed the women with his extensive knowledge of gardening plants. In turn, the women peppered him with questions, which he didn't seem to mind answering.

Kate excused Blossom and Izzy from clean-up duty so they could return to their card game. Shelby cleared the table and stored leftovers while Kate and Josh attacked the dishes. They worked at the sink with their heads close together, so deep in conversation Shelby didn't dare interrupt them.

Shelby thanked him when she walked him to his car afterward. "You're a good sport for putting up with them."

He scoffed at her, "Are you kidding? I loved it. I've always enjoyed old people. I find them way more interesting than people our age, present company excluded."

She laughed. "They have an unfair advantage. They've lived longer than we have, which makes them much wiser. What was my mom talking to you about while you were doing the dishes? You two seemed so serious."

"She asked me some questions about running my business. I got the impression she's considering a venture."

Shelby nodded. "She designs light fixtures. She's really talented too." She held up her hands to show her crossed fingers. "I hope you've inspired her to proceed with her plan."

twenty-nine

. . .

After being alone all week, Grace dreaded the long evening
ahead. *Why not go out? It is Thursday night, after all.*

Around four thirty, she posted in her group text to her
girlfriends.

> Anyone have plans for tonight?

Several friends immediately responded about a party Tasha
was having for Brent's birthday.

Alison sent Grace a separate text.

> Tasha invited a few people over at the last
> minute. I'm sure she wouldn't mind if you
> stopped by.

Alison was Grace's closest friend and maid of honor. She was
politely informing Grace that she was not invited to save her from
making a fool of herself.

Grace drummed her fingers on her desk. She had never been
excluded from anything in her life. As Brent's best friend, Wyatt
would be invited to the party. Naturally, Grace would be included
in the invitation. Unsure of the party's start time, she waited until

six to leave work. Making a quick stop at the liquor store for a bottle of whiskey for Brent, she arrived at their house at six thirty. Cars were parked in the driveway and along the side of the street. Walking toward the house, she heard live music coming from their backyard. This sounded like more than an impromptu party.

Grace paused at the front door. Should she ring the bell? She usually just walked on in. She'd no sooner stepped inside the foyer than Tasha pulled her into the dining room away from the other guests.

"What're you doing here?" Tasha asked in a loud whisper.

Grace's heart sank. She'd been wrong. She wasn't invited after all. "I came to wish Brent a happy birthday," she said, holding up the whiskey gift bag.

"Wyatt specifically asked me not to invite you. Surely you understand why I have to take sides."

Grace's hair stood on end. "Actually, I don't understand. Why would you take sides?"

Tasha leaned in close. "You were living together, engaged to be married. Your breakup is like a divorce. One of you will get the house, the other the friends. And since most of your friends are Wyatt's, it looks like you're getting the house," she said with a malicious grin.

Grace shook her head in disbelief. "Wait! What? We didn't break up. We're just having a little disagreement about the wedding."

"Sounded like more than a little disagreement to me. He called you a Diva-zilla," Tasha said, pressing her fingers to her lips to hide her smile. "You have to admit, it is kinda funny."

Brent cleared his throat as he entered the dining room. "What's going on in here?"

Grace handed him the gift bag. "I stopped by to wish you a happy birthday."

"That was thoughtful of you. Thanks," he said, taking the bag and kissing Grace's cheek.

Grace shifted her weight, avoiding Brent's intense gaze. "Well,

I should probably get going. According to Tasha, I wasn't invited."

Brent gave his wife a scolding look. "Don't go yet! I treated myself to a killer classic rock band. You'll love them. They're taking a break right now, but they'll start playing again soon."

Grace smiled at Brent. He knew she was a huge fan of classic rock. "All right. I'll stay for one drink."

"Excellent." Brent motioned her to go ahead of him out of the dining room. As they walked together toward the back of the house, he said, "For the record, Wyatt told me in confidence about your breakup. My wife was eavesdropping on our conversation, and she blabbed the news to everyone. Tasha and I are in a big fight about it. You and I have been friends for a long time, Grace. I hope you and Wyatt can work things out."

"Thanks for saying that, Brent. It really means a lot."

As they emerged from the house, Brent excused himself to speak to a friend, and Grace made her way through the crowd to the bar. She grabbed a margarita, the party's signature drink, and stood awkwardly by herself. Was it her imagination or was everyone staring at her? Snippets of conversation floated through the air, but when she heard someone use the term Diva-zilla, she knew they were all talking about her.

Grace had shunned countless people in her life, but she'd never been on the wrong side of ostracism. And she was surprised by how much it hurt. She eyed her escape. In order to get to the back door, she would have to retrace her steps through the crowd. Everyone would see her leaving in disgrace.

Alison appeared at her side. "Ignore these jerks. They'll have their laugh, and then move on to some other poor subject tomorrow."

Tears blurred Grace's vision as she looked down at the bluestone terrace. "I just want to get out of here."

"I can help with that." Alison hooked her arm through Grace's. "Come inside with me. I need to use the restroom," she said, loud enough for everyone to hear as they passed through the crowd.

Alison walked her through the house and out the front door. "I talked to Wyatt. I can tell he's hurting."

Grace dug through her purse for a tissue. "We've been arguing about the wedding, but I didn't realize he considered us broken up."

"He says you've changed, and he's worried you won't go back to being the old Grace after you're married."

Grace rolled her eyes as she dabbed at her tears. "He's being ridiculous. I haven't changed."

"Maybe you should try talking to him again. I'm sure you can work out a compromise."

"Maybe." Grace pressed her cheek to Alison's. "Thanks for rescuing me," she said and hurried to her car.

Grace sped through the neighboring streets to the safety of her home. By compromising, she would be setting a dangerous precedent for their marriage. She needed to set expectations. Wyatt needed to know who was in charge.

On a whim, Kate stopped by Myrtle's Bed and Breakfast on her way home from running errands Friday morning. She spotted Myrtle on the front porch, speaking with a guest, and waved to the long-time family friend.

"I'm going to check out your garden," she called out to Myrtle. "I hear it's spectacular."

Myrtle smiled and gave her a thumbs-up.

Shelby was right. *Enchanted* was the perfect word to describe the charming garden. To maximize space, her backyard was divided into quaint garden rooms. Each nook was aesthetically pleasing and filled with the intoxicating aroma of roses in bloom.

Josh and his sister were artists in their own right. Kate, likewise, considered herself an artist. She'd long since outgrown her role as salesperson. While she found the idea of co-managing the resort with her brother intriguing, she needed to create to be fulfilled. But she couldn't imagine a role in the new resort that would foster her creativity.

Kate spent the remainder of the afternoon on the beach with a legal pad and pen, working out a budget for a scaled-down version of Grace's dream wedding, leaving herself ample money to start her lighting business.

Now all she had to do was convince Grace. Anticipating fireworks, she didn't dare call her daughter while Grace was at work. At six o'clock, Kate poured herself a glass of wine and took it out to the pool.

Grace answered the call with an abrupt, "Yes, Mother."

"Are you okay, sweetheart? Did I catch you at a bad time?"

"I'm perfectly fine," Grace snapped. "Is there a reason you called?"

"I . . . um . . ." Kate wondered if she should wait until her daughter was in a better mood to present her idea. Then again, she couldn't let her daughter's moods dictate her life. "I've come up with a budget for your wedding. If we streamline our expenses, we can have a perfectly lovely reception," she said and briefly outlined her ideas for cutting costs.

"Maybe if you and Dad combine your resources, we can have the big wedding."

Kate gripped the phone. "Are you willing to wait five years to get married? Because your father isn't currently in a position to pay for any of it. Our financial circumstances have drastically changed. Unfortunately, that means our lifestyles will have to change accordingly."

"This is so unfair, Mom. I'm being punished because you and Dad are poor money managers."

Kate's muscles tensed, and her body went rigid. "For your information, Grace, I've been saving my money for years to start a lighting company. Because I know how much this wedding means to you, I'm willing to use a portion of that money to pay for it."

"A portion? How generous of you. You're a salesperson. What do you know about running your own company anyway? Didn't you learn anything from Dad's botched venture?"

Kate's jaw hit the table. "I beg your pardon."

"You heard me," Grace said in a steely tone.

Kate inhaled a steadying breath. "I am still your mother, and you will not speak to me that way. I did not raise you to be so insensitive and self-absorbed. For days, I've worried myself sick about paying for your wedding. And your ungratefulness is the thanks I get. You're making plenty of money. You can pay for the wedding yourself," she said and hung up.

Kate sank back in her chair, taking a gulp of wine. She had vastly underestimated her daughter's resolve. Yet, Kate was at fault for overindulging her eldest child. Grace had always been an overachiever. To reward Grace for her many accomplishments, Kate had granted her every desire. In the process, she'd created a monster.

thirty

. . .

G race dropped her phone on the counter with a clatter.
"Good job, Grace. Now you've alienated your only ally."
She picked up the phone again and texted her father.

> Any chance you're free for golf in the morning?
> We could grab lunch in the grill room afterward.

He responded right away.

> Sorry sweetheart. I'm working tomorrow.

> I could come to the hospital. We could eat in the
> cafeteria.

Grace was desperate. The thought of cafeteria food made her
want to barf.

> I'll be in surgery most of the day. Another time?

Surgery? On a Saturday? Grace smelled a skunk. A skunk
named Claudia. Grace didn't bother responding.

Grace spent a lonely evening in front of the television with a bag of popcorn and a bottle of wine. She rose early on Saturday, put on her bathing suit, and packed a tote bag for the pool. The first to arrive, she chose a lounge chair in the center of the pool deck where her friends couldn't ignore her. But when the pool began to fill up, the chairs on either side of her remained empty.

A hungover-looking Brent and Wyatt sat on the opposite side of the pool, sipping Bloody Marys with their feet hanging over the side. She was sure Wyatt saw her, yet he looked everywhere but at her.

Disheartened, she left the pool before noon. She was on her way to the parking lot when she spotted her father and Claudia getting into a golf cart. She was right. Her father's new girlfriend was a skunk.

At home, she closed all the shades and set the thermostat to sixty degrees. Wrapping herself in a blanket, she curled up on the sofa with a bottle of vodka and the TV remote. She didn't leave the sofa for the rest of the day except to go pee. She passed out at some point that night, and she woke on Sunday morning to find the vodka bottle empty. She ordered another through Uber Eats and set to work on it.

Her life in Austin was ruined. She'd have to move to another town where she knew no one, where she was a nobody. She'd never find another guy like Wyatt. He wasn't perfect, but he understood her. At least, he used to. Perhaps he was the one who had changed.

Kate was heartsick over her argument with Grace. She'd lost her husband, her best friend, and now her oldest daughter. She was rethinking everything about her life, including her decision to make the Lowcountry her permanent home and her desire to start her own business. She even questioned her logic in leaving Rand until she reminded herself that he cheated on her with her best friend.

She avoided her family over the weekend. She didn't want to drag them down with her gloomy mood. On Sunday afternoon, after the weekend guests had departed, she sequestered herself under an umbrella in a remote corner of the pool deck with her legal pad. She was deep in thought, her pen flying across the page, when Pritchard plopped down on the empty lounge chair beside her.

"What're you doing, sis?"

"Making task lists to get my business up and running." She dropped the legal pad onto her lap and looked up at him. "What're *you* doing?"

"I just stopped by to check on things. I'm leaving in the morning for Nashville. I'll only be gone a couple of days. I've hired a moving company to clear out my apartment." Pritchard eyed the legal pad. "So you've decided to move forward with Lumina Designs?"

"I haven't pulled the trigger yet, but I'm close. I'm terrified, Pritchard. My savings is all I have left. If my lighting company doesn't make it, I'm broke."

"You're a St. Clair, Kate. You'll never be broke as long as we own this property," he said, pointing at the ground. "If things don't work out, you'll co-manage the resort with me." He stretched out his legs on the lounge chair and crossed his ankles. "Besides, my offer to purchase your fixtures for the resort is the rocket you need to launch your company. I aim to make The Sanctuary a showplace. People will be lining up at your door to order your fixtures."

Kate smiled at her brother. "I'm grateful for the opportunity, Pritchard. Your faith in me means a lot. I promise not to let you down."

"I know you won't." He closed his eyes and tilted his face to the sky. "What did you decide about Grace's wedding?"

"I spoke to her on Friday afternoon, and I offered to pay for a wedding that I can afford. The conversation didn't go well."

"You did the right thing, Kate. Don't worry. Grace will come around," Pritchard said with more conviction than Kate felt.

Later in the day, Kate was strolling on the beach when Jolene appeared at her feet. She knelt to pet the wet, sandy dog. A shadow crossed her line of sight, and she looked up at Blossom. "Hey there!"

"Hey, yourself. Where have you been all weekend? If I didn't know better, I'd think you were avoiding me," Blossom said with a cackle of laughter.

Kate straightened. "I've been avoiding everyone. Grace and I had a terrible argument on Friday. I've been in a lousy mood since then."

Blossom's smile faded. "I'm sorry, Katie girl. Do you want to talk about it?"

Kate shrugged. "There's not much to tell," she said, briefly summarizing her conversation with Grace.

Blossom grimaced. "Ouch. Sounds like she's hurting and lashing out at you."

Kate shielded her eyes from the sun. "What do you mean? Why would she be hurting?"

"For any number of reasons. Maybe she's reacting to your separation from your husband. Divorce is always hard on kids, no matter their age. Or maybe something's going on with her at work. Who knows? She could be fighting with her fiancé."

"I didn't think of that. What do I do? Should I call her and ask if something is troubling her?"

Blossom shook her head. "Not yet. I would wait a few days. See if she comes to you first. Your fight may be weighing heavily on her as well."

Kate started walking, and Blossom fell into line beside her. "I'm furious with her, Blossom. What if she does come to me? Am I supposed to just forgive her?"

"Yep. You welcome her with open arms, be the bigger person, suck up your pride for the sake of your relationship."

In other words, she would have to forget the hurtful things Grace said. And she wasn't sure she could do that. "Why is parenting so difficult?"

"*Mothering* is difficult. Fathers have it easy. Most don't have the stomachs for drama. They leave the ugly work to us."

Kate chuckled. Rand had always insisted Kate be the disciplinarian and bearer of difficult conversations with their children. "You're right about that."

Blossom picked up her dog. "I need to give this wet mess a bath. If you're heading home, we can walk together."

"I have some more thinking to do. I'm going to walk a little farther."

Blossom tucked the squirming dog under her arm. "I don't blame you. It's a beautiful afternoon. I enjoy Sundays when the guests leave, and Magnolia Shores quiets down after the weekend. I made some shrimp salad for dinner if you care to join me."

"That sounds delicious. And thanks for the pep talk, Blossom."

"Anytime, love bug."

Kate replayed the conversation in her mind as she continued north. When she reached the Sandy Island Club, she stopped walking and stared down at her phone. What if Blossom was right? What if Grace was going through a rough patch? She yearned to call Grace to apologize. But coddling her oldest daughter would do her a disservice. Grace had said some hurtful things. She needed to be the one to apologize first. The waiting was interminable. This was what tough love felt like.

Kate reminded herself that her children were grown. Her old life was over. It was now time for her to chart her future. Turning back toward home, she clicked on Ethan's number. He answered right away.

"If you're still interested, I'm ready to move forward with Lumina Designs," she said.

He let out a whoop of excitement. "Let's go!"

His enthusiasm brought a smile to her face. "Yes! Let's! Are you free for dinner tomorrow night?"

"Sorry. I can't tomorrow. I have a client event. How about Tuesday? I'll come to Water's Edge."

"Perfect. In the meantime, I'll interview some realtors," Kate said.

"And I'll reach out to an attorney friend about forming our partnership."

They talked for a minute more about dinner plans before hanging up.

Kate's spirits soared, and she increased her pace. She'd been given a new beginning.

Welcome to your life Part Two, Kate St. Clair.

She felt more confident in her decision than she had about anything in her life. She was on her way, and there was no turning back now.

thirty-one

. . .

G race reported a mild case of COVID to senior management on Monday morning and made arrangements to work from home for the rest of the week. But she struggled to focus on work. Her life hadn't always been a bed of roses. She'd suffered a few disappointments along the way. But she'd always bounced back quickly. Then again, the stakes had never been this high. Her body ached for Wyatt. She didn't feel whole without him, and she feared she'd lost him for good. But her guilt over her fight with her mother was eating her up inside.

She stayed in bed most of the day, sleeping off her weekend hangover, but then she struggled to fall asleep at bedtime. She longed for a shot of vodka to take the edge off her frayed nerves. But she'd finished the last bottle yesterday and wouldn't allow herself to order more. Alcohol would not solve her problems. Unfortunately, she was at a loss for what would.

Around three in the morning, she gave up trying to sleep and went to the kitchen for coffee. She sat down with her laptop and booked the first available flight to Charleston, leaving Austin at eleven thirty and arriving a few minutes after four. For the next few hours, she caught up on work. Then she showered, packed, and headed out to the airport.

Grace arrived at Magnolia Shores to find that annoying woman, Blossom, seated at the reception desk. Blossom's little dog circled Grace's feet, growling at her.

"Easy, Tiger," Grace said to the dog. She looked up at Blossom. "He doesn't bite, does he?"

"He is a she. As far as I know, she's never bitten anyone. But we've only been together a couple of months," Blossom said with a smirk tugging at her lips.

Unsure if she was joking, Grace decided not to respond. "Where's my mom?" she asked.

"She's having dinner in town with her new business partner."

"Oh," Grace said, disappointed. "What about my sister? Is she here?"

"Shelby went to meet her new boyfriend's parents. I'm covering for her. Can I help you with something?" Blossom asked, folding her hands on the desk.

"Do you know if there are any rooms available?"

Blossom gestured at the computer. "Sorry. I don't know how to work that thing. I'm sure there probably are. It's been quiet around here yesterday and today. But you'll have to wait for Kate or Shelby to return." Blossom eased herself out of the chair and came from behind the desk. "Are you hungry? I was getting ready to grill a chicken breast and make a salad. I have enough for two."

Grace hadn't eaten a real meal in days. "Sure. I could eat." She left her suitcase at the bottom of the stairs and followed Blossom into the kitchen. On the island, beside an empty wooden salad bowl, was a plate with two delicious-looking grilled chicken breasts. With furrowed brow, Grace looked from the chicken to Blossom. "You said you were *getting ready* to grill the chicken."

Blossom winked at her. "My rapid cooking method is faster than the speed of sound. Watch," she said and snapped her fingers.

Grace blinked. When she looked again at the island, the wooden salad bowl was filled with lush lettuce greens. She shook her head in bewilderment. "I don't even want to know how you just did that."

Blossom went to the refrigerator. "Would you like a glass of white wine or sweet tea?"

"Sweet tea, please." Grace was officially on the wagon. After all the vodka she'd consumed the past few days, she might never come off.

They sat down together at the table, and Blossom offered the blessing. Jabbing her fork at her salad, Blossom asked, "What's new with you, sunshine? I didn't expect to see you again so soon."

Grace had never been one to confide in friends, let alone a perfect stranger. But she found herself pouring her heart out to Blossom about her breakup with Wyatt, her fight with her mother, and her father choosing to play golf with his new girlfriend instead of Grace. "My life is such a mess. I don't know how to make things right. Tell me what to do, Blossom." Pushing her plate away, Grace buried her face in her hands and cried.

Blossom moved her chair closer to Grace, placing an arm around her waist. "Don't cry, sunshine. All is not lost. You can still make amends if you choose to do so?"

"How?" Grace sobbed.

Blossom smoothed Grace's hair back from her face. "First, you must decide what it is you truly want."

"I want to marry Wyatt. If only we could agree on the wedding."

"You mean, if only *he* agrees to *your* wedding."

Grace looked at her in surprise. How did she know Grace and Wyatt were fighting over the wedding? Must be part of her job as . . . What was she again? A guardian angel?

"Why is having a big wedding so important to you?" When Grace hesitated, Blossom added, "Tell the truth now. I'll know if you're lying."

"Of course you will." Grace hung her head. "What's so wrong with wanting my moment in the limelight?"

"You said the operative word. Your wedding is a single *moment* in a lifetime of *moments*. A ninety-year-old person lives two billion, eight hundred thirty-seven million, four hundred forty thousand moments. If you're blessed to have a happy marriage for fifty years, that's one billion, five hundred seventy-six million, eight hundred thousand moments."

Grace's hand shot out. "Okay! Stop! I get your point."

"Are you willing to risk losing Wyatt over this single moment?"

Grace slumped back in her chair. "I honestly don't care about the wedding anymore. I just want to be his wife. I don't even want to wait until April. I'm fine with eloping. Whatever he wants. I'm even warming up to the idea of having a kid right away."

"Do you really mean that?"

Grace sat up straight in her chair. "I do! With my whole heart. I just don't know how to make it happen. Wyatt won't believe me if I tell him all that. He'll think I'm caving just to get him back."

"What if you *showed* him you mean it instead?"

Grace scrunched up her nose. "Like how?"

"Like, invite him to his own wedding. You have everything you need to get married right here at Magnolia Shores. I have the authority to officiate. We can find someone to cater a small luncheon. Your family is already here. Invite him down for the weekend and marry him. You can send him one of those computer invitation thingamajigs."

Grace thought about the small wedding two weeks ago. Sally and Bobby had seemed so happy, surrounded by their family and close friends. "That's a brilliant idea, Blossom. But at this late date, I doubt any rooms are available for the weekend."

"You'd have to confirm with your sister, but I'm pretty sure I overheard her say a small group had just canceled for the weekend."

Grace jumped to her feet. "Cool! Let me get my laptop. I'll send out the invitation."

Retrieving the laptop from her bag in the foyer, she brought it back to the table and accessed the Evite website. Over the years, she'd sent countless electronic invitations for various events, and she knew how to navigate the website. She chose a simple wedding design with a watercolor eucalyptus wreath and added her and Wyatt's names. "Should I set the date for this weekend?"

"Why not? Put Saturday's date on the invitation. Your eagerness will get your man's attention. If it doesn't work out and no rooms are available, you could pick a later date that suits you both."

"His parents are in Europe. They're coming back soon, but I'm not exactly sure when." She typed in the rest of the information and shifted the computer so Blossom could see it.

Blossom nodded her approval. "It's lovely. Are you going to send it?"

Grace made a few minor tweaks. "I'm not sure. It's a big step. I should talk to Mama first," she said, her mouse hovering over the Send button.

"You're in luck. She just pulled into the driveway."

Grace's head snapped back. "What? I didn't hear a car. How do you know that?" She smiled. "Never mind. I already know. Your magical powers are at work again."

Kate floated across the courtyard, still riding high on Champagne bubbles. Ethan had insisted they toast the birth of Lumina Designs, though they limited themselves to just one glass since they were both driving.

Her spirits deflated when she saw Grace seated at the kitchen table with Blossom. Something must be terribly wrong for her daughter to fly back to South Carolina so soon.

Grace shot out of her chair and rushed over to Kate, throwing her arms around her. "Mama! I'm so sorry for the awful things I said on the phone. Wyatt and I have been arguing, and I wasn't in my right mind."

Kate winked at Blossom over her daughter's shoulder. She'd been right. Grace and Wyatt had been fighting. She wrapped her arms around her daughter, holding her tight. "I'm sorry too, sweetheart. We've all suffered a major shock. Adjusting to our new circumstances will take some time. We must be patient with one another." She held Grace at arm's length. "Have you and Wyatt made up?"

Before Grace could answer, Shelby appeared in the opposite doorway from the front hall. "What's going on? Why are you here, Grace? Did someone die?"

Grace pushed away from Kate. "Don't be ridiculous, Shelby. Mom and I had a disagreement, and I came to apologize." She turned back to Kate. "To answer your question, Wyatt and I have been fighting about our wedding. He wants a small wedding, and he thinks I let things get out of hand. And he's right. Blossom came up with the brilliant idea for us to get married here this weekend."

Shelby appeared mortified. "Here? As in Magnolia Shores?"

"Yes, here. If there are any rooms available," Grace said in a hopeful tone as she locked eyes with her sister.

"We only have four rooms available," Shelby said. "I guess you'll have to wait until another time. Like never."

Grace ignored her sister's sarcasm. "Four works." She ticked the rooms off her fingers. "One for Wyatt's parents. Wyatt and I will share one. I'm not sure about Brent yet. And Dad, although I doubt he comes. Can you hold them for us?"

"Only until noon tomorrow," Shelby said.

"I should know by then. I'm sending Wyatt an invitation to our wedding." Grace crossed her hands over her chest and batted her eyelashes. "Isn't that so romantic? Another one of Blossom's ideas."

"He'll probably say no," Shelby said, crossing the room to the back door. "I'm going to bed."

"Wait! Where should I sleep tonight?" Grace asked.

"Room three in the garden house is open. The key is on the

board behind the desk," Shelby said, slamming the door behind her.

"Excuse me a minute." Kate followed her younger daughter outside, hurrying to catch up with Shelby in the courtyard. "Shelby? How did your evening with Josh's parents go?"

"Good. They are incredibly nice people," Shelby said in a short tone.

"What's wrong, sweetheart? You don't seem like yourself," Kate said, fingering a lock of Shelby's strawberry-blonde hair.

Shelby brushed her hand away. "I'm irritated that Grace is here. Leave it to her to upend our lives by having her wedding this weekend."

"Oh, honey. Can't you be nice to your sister, just this once? After everything we've been through, our family needs this healing time together."

"I'm not the one preventing the healing, Mom. By the way, I have to work on Saturday. I won't be attending the wedding," Shelby said and stormed off toward the pool house.

When Kate returned to the kitchen, Grace looked up from her computer. "Are you okay with this, Mom? I need your approval before I send him this invitation," she said, her pointer finger poised over the return button on her keyboard.

Kate nodded. "I wholeheartedly approve, sweetheart." Secretly, she was thrilled at this latest development. She would no longer have to fork over a chunk of her savings for a lavish wedding.

Grace clicked the button. "Done. Now we wait for him to respond."

"We have a lot of planning to do," Kate said, filling a kettle with water. "Does anyone want tea?"

"I do," Blossom and Grace said in unison.

Kate steeped three mugs of chamomile tea and joined them at the table. "So, tell me how you see this wedding."

"Simple. Family only. A late-morning ceremony on the terrace followed by lunch," Grace said, her eyes on her computer screen.

"We'll need a caterer and florist," Kate said.

Grace planted her elbows on the table. "I'll need a dress. What will I wear?"

"We can try the bridal boutiques in Charleston. Maybe they have a sample dress they can alter in time. If not, you may have to settle for something else—maybe a fun maxi dress. You can wear whatever you want for your impromptu wedding. We'll need to go shopping tomorrow though. I'm meeting with a realtor at eight to look at a potential warehouse for my business. We can leave right after that."

Grace slammed her computer shut. "That works for me. If Wyatt says yes. But what if he says no? Why hasn't he responded?"

"He'll say yes. He's probably sleeping," Blossom suggested.

Grace checked the time on her Apple Watch. "I doubt it. It's only nine o'clock in Texas." She pushed back from the table. "I'm tired too. I'm going to my room."

Grace kissed the top of Kate's head. "Good night, Mama." She grinned at Blossom. "Thank you, Blossom. I was wrong about you. I really like your style."

Blossom winked at Grace. "I was wrong about you too, sunshine."

thirty-two

· · ·

Grace stayed awake half the night, awaiting Wyatt's response to her invitation. Her exhausted brain imagined the worst. He'd found someone else. He no longer loved her, no longer wanted to marry her. She'd pushed him away. Was it too late to get him back?

It was after three before she finally dozed off. Her ringing phone on the pillow beside her head woke her at seven the next morning. The sight of Wyatt's image on the screen made her sit bolt upright in bed. "Good morning," she said to Wyatt.

"Morning, Grace. I'm calling to respond to your very clever invitation. Do you mean it though? Is this what you really want?"

"Yes! I don't care about the wedding. All I want is to be married to you, Wyatt. I made some terrible mistakes. I've been selfish and inconsiderate. I hope you can forgive me."

"I forgive you. I just want the old Grace back."

Grace ran her fingers through her knotted hair. "I admit I've been acting like a Diva-zilla lately. Almost losing you taught me a lot of very valuable lessons."

"I've been pretty miserable myself without you. We could just have a small wedding. Either there or here. We don't have to rush."

"I prefer to think of it as impromptu," Grace said, adopting the word her mother had used last night. "I'd love to do it this weekend, but I understand if you need time to think about it."

Wyatt didn't hesitate. "I'm all in. I think it'll be a ton of fun. But I'll need to clear it with my parents first. They arrived home from Europe last night."

"Great! I couldn't remember when they were due back." Grace's heart soared. This was actually happening. She was getting married this weekend. "In South Carolina, we have to wait twenty-four hours after applying for our marriage license, so you should come as soon as possible."

"That means I will need to fly in tonight. Let me talk to my parents. I'll call you back in a minute."

Grace lowered herself to the edge of the bed, watching the minutes click off the clock on the nightstand. After ten minutes, she grew antsy and stepped outside to the balcony for fresh air. She was working herself into a panic attack, imagining his parents' disapproval, when the call finally came through.

"I'm sorry that took so long," Wyatt said. "They're jetlagged. I had to call several times before they picked up. When I told them we are getting married this weekend, they immediately assumed you are pregnant. But I assured them we simply don't want to wait until April to be married. Mom was booking their flights for Friday when we hung up."

Grace collapsed against the balcony. "Yay! I'm super excited."

"Me too, babe! What do you want your groom to wear?"

"Hmm." Grace chewed on her thumbnail. "Your navy sport coat and casual pants. We only have four available rooms. Do you think Brent will come?"

"I'll ask. I'm not sure he can get away on such short notice."

"I can't believe this. I have so much to do today," Grace said, going back inside the room.

"Same. Let me get a move-on. I'll text you my flight itinerary."

When she hung up, Grace texted her mother.

Wyatt accepted my invitation. We're getting married on Saturday. I'll be ready to go to Charleston when you finish your meeting.

———

Sadie Holloway was technically a residential real estate agent, but her long-time client had insisted on listing their warehouse with her. The space was perfect for a budding lighting company, with a large room in the back for production, a smaller showroom out front, and several offices on the second floor. It was located on the main highway a couple of miles outside of town, allowing for easy access for future clients. The property had been on the market for over six months, and Sadie assured them the owners were motivated to sell.

After the showing, Kate and Ethan huddled together beside Kate's car while they determined their asking price. Kate explained to Ethan about Grace's wedding. "I don't want to wait to make our offer, but I may be difficult to reach the next few days."

Ethan smiled. "So your daughter came to her senses. That's so exciting. I hope all goes well." He opened her car door. "You go ahead. I'll convey our asking price to Sadie and have her submit the offer."

"You're the best, Ethan. I promise my life will settle down soon."

"I'm not worried about a thing, girlfriend. If you're not too tired from the wedding, I'd like to meet again on Sunday afternoon to divvy up duties."

"Deal!" Kate said, offering him a high five. "Have a good weekend, partner."

"Same. Congrats to the bride and groom."

Grace was waiting for her on the front stoop at Magnolia Shores. She got in the car, and they headed off to Charleston.

"We have so much to do. Let's start with finding a florist."

Kate handed Grace her phone. "You place the calls, and we'll talk to them on speaker."

They spoke with every florist in town, and even though they only needed a bridal bouquet and a table arrangement, none could accommodate them on such short notice. They had the same bad luck with a caterer.

"Maybe we should wait until later in the summer to get married," Grace said, dejected.

Kate shook her head. "That's not an option. The bed and breakfast is booked every weekend until Labor Day. How many people do you think we'll have for lunch?"

Grace counted on her fingers. "Thirteen. Fifteen max, depending on whether Dad and Brent come."

"We can easily prepare a simple meal for that many. I should let Pritchard know about the wedding." Kate took her phone from Grace and clicked on her brother's number. When his voice filled the car, she asked, "How's the move going?"

"Coming along," Pritchard said. "Everything is almost out of the apartment. We'll be heading back to South Carolina soon."

"What will you do with all your furniture?"

"Put it in storage for now. Harper and Cody have made an offer on a house. If they get it, they'll be able to use a lot of this stuff."

"That's exciting. I wish them luck." She glanced over at Grace. "I have some exciting news of my own," she said and told him about the wedding. "Grace is in the car with me now. We're heading to Charleston now to look for a dress. I hope you and Savannah can come, as well as Harper and Cody. The ceremony is at eleven, with lunch following. Although, since we can't find a caterer, we may be serving a Chick-fil-A platter."

"We'll be there. Why don't you let Savannah and me handle the food?"

"That's a lot, Pritchard. I can't ask you to do that."

"You're not asking. I'm offering. No, I'm insisting. Seriously, we would love to do this for you. We'll be in charge of decorating the table as well."

Kate glanced over at Grace, who gave her a thumbs-up. "We accept," Kate said.

"Thanks so much, Pritchard," Grace added.

"Does anyone have a seafood allergy?" Pritchard asked.

Kate frowned. "Not that I know of."

"We're all good," Grace said.

They talked a minute more about the menu before ending the call.

Grace stared down at her phone. "I guess I need to call Dad. What should I do about Claudia?"

Kate gripped the steering wheel. "That's your call, sweetheart. But I would prefer it if she didn't come."

"Me too." Grace's call went to voicemail, and she left a message for her father. "Hey, Dad. It's Grace. Wyatt and I are getting married this weekend at Magnolia Shores. And no, I'm not pregnant. I would love you to give me away, but Claudia isn't invited. I'm sure you can understand why. Call me back when you get this."

Five minutes later, Grace's phone pinged. "This is from Dad." Tears filled her eyes as she read the message out loud. "Sorry, honey. I can't make it this weekend. You'll make a lovely bride."

Kate reached for Grace's hand. "I'm sorry, Grace. This isn't about you. Your father has disappointed a lot of people lately. Most of all himself. His stubborn pride won't let him show his face."

"You give him too much credit, Mom. He's not coming because he can't bring Claudia."

The shopping expedition yielded zero results. Not a single wedding gown, cocktail dress, or maxi appealed to her. An increasingly desperate Grace would've purchased a white dress pantsuit if she had found one she liked.

Wyatt's flight schedule played in their favor, enabling them to pick him up at the Charleston airport on their way out of town. When she saw him standing on the curb with his suitcase, Grace hopped out of the car and threw her arms around him. Ignoring the bustling travelers around them, he kissed her with more passion than he had in months.

Grace insisted he sit beside her mother in the front passenger seat to allow for more legroom for his tall frame.

"So how are the wedding preparations coming?" he asked as Kate navigated out of the airport.

"Pritchard and Savannah are taking charge of the lunch," Grace explained. "But all the florists are booked, and I didn't find a dress today."

He shifted in his seat to see her. "We can always postpone, Grace."

"No way! We're getting married this weekend. I'll wear my bathing suit if I have to."

"Yes!" Wyatt said, punching the air. "The old Grace is back. You'll look amazing in your bathing suit, and if need be, I'll buy you a bouquet of wilted carnations from the grocery store."

Kate cut her eyes at him. "You'll do no such thing. I'll cut every blue hydrangea bloom off Izzy's prized bushes before I let my daughter carry a bouquet of carnations on her wedding day."

"I stand corrected," Wyatt said, and they all laughed.

When they arrived at Magnolia Shores, Izzy and Blossom were in the kitchen cooking dinner. They stopped what they were doing to welcome the groom.

"You're adorable," Blossom said, pinching his cheek and making Wyatt blush.

He hugged Izzy, whom he'd known for years. "I'm glad to see you, Izzy. You gave us quite the scare when you had the stroke."

Izzy let out a humph. "I'm too mean to die. Now, please marry this girl and take her off our hands."

"Izzy!" Grace scoffed. "Gosh! I'm not that bad."

"I'm just joking. You're a wonderful girl," Izzy said, looping her arm through Grace's. "After all, you're *my* granddaughter."

"That I am." Grace looked over at Blossom. "Can you please wave your magic wand? We need a florist and a wedding dress."

"I can handle the flowers," Blossom said. "Do you like blue hydrangeas?"

"I love them. They're my favorite," Grace said.

"Mine too." Blossom winked at Izzy. "Don't worry. I won't rob your bushes. I have an inside source," she said and let out a hearty laugh.

An idea struck Grace. As a child, she'd spent untold hours staring at her mother's wedding portrait, standing prominently on the corner table in their family room. She remembered her gown being elegantly simple. "Where is your wedding dress, Mom? Is there any chance I could wear it?"

Kate let out a huff. "That old thing? It's stuffed in the back of a closet somewhere, yellowed with age."

Izzy clapped her hands. "Actually, it's not. It's under my bed in the cottage. I had it professionally cleaned and preserved. It should be in good shape."

Kate gave Grace a once-over. "I was about your size back then, so it should fit."

Tingles of excitement fluttered across Grace's chest. "Can I try it on?"

Izzy's face lit up. "Yes! Of course. Let's go take a look."

The four women bustled toward the back door with Grace saying over her shoulder to Wyatt, "You and I are staying in room three in the garden house. Make yourself at home. I'll be there in a few."

In the cottage, Kate dragged the big white box out from beneath her mother's bed and gingerly removed the dress—a strapless gown in creamy satin with a fitted drop waist.

Grace's blue eyes widened. "It's more gorgeous in person. I hope it fits," she said, stripping off her clothes.

Blossom held Grace's arm while she stepped into the dress. Kate zipped the zipper, and Izzy closed the door, revealing a full-length mirror. Grace admired her reflection, pivoting in a circle to look at the back. "I love it."

Her mother pressed her fingers to her lips, her eyes shiny with unshed tears. "You're stunning. The dress is perfect for you."

"Do you still have your veil?" Grace asked.

Izzy checked the box. "Yes, here it is."

She passed the veil—a two-layered shoulder-length tulle piece attached to a pearl headband—to Kate, who secured it onto Grace's head.

Blossom folded her hands over her chest. "Your man's eyes will fall out of his head when he sees you."

Izzy and Kate hummed their agreement. "We couldn't have found a dress better suited for the bride or the occasion," Kate said.

Grace's throat thickened. "I agree. I'm thrilled. Thank you, Izzy, for having it preserved."

Izzy smiled softly. "You're most welcome."

Kate clasped her hands together. "Dress, check. Flowers, check. Food, check. Groom, check. Looks like we've got ourselves a wedding."

thirty-three

. . .

The rowdy celebratory dinner in the kitchen drove Shelby out of the house and down to the dock. Leaning against a piling, she opened Elin Hildebrand's summer release and peeled off a protein bar wrapper. As she heard the rumble of an outboard motor, she looked up with anticipation, hoping to see Josh, only to find Matt's boat approaching instead.

Pulling up alongside the dock, he said, "Hey, Shelby. What're you up to?"

She waved the book at him. "Reading. Avoiding my family. My sister decided to get married here this weekend, and everyone is in an uproar. What're you doing?"

"Just out for a ride," he said, tying his line in a figure eight around a cleat.

She set down her book and swung her legs over the end of the dock. "Where's Ada?"

"At work, I guess. I haven't talked to her in days. Our relationship has fizzled."

"Why? Is she not perfect enough for you?"

Matt got off the boat and sat down beside her. "Ada's great. The problem is, I can't stop thinking about you. You're in my head, Shelby. I've never felt this way about anyone before."

Shelby's heart skipped a beat. "What about our age difference?"

"In hindsight, I was using that as an excuse to avoid facing my feelings for you. I think I'm falling in love with you. Would you consider giving us another chance?"

Shelby hesitated. Was he serious? Another chance? Wasn't this what she wanted? But she found herself saying, "I'm sorry, Matt. But I'm dating Josh now. He's reliable and considerate, and he treats me like I'm the most special person on the planet."

Matt flashed Shelby a boyish grin. "But does he make you melt like I do?"

She glared at him. "Please leave. I'm not in a good mood."

"I'm sorry, Shelby. I didn't mean to upset you. Will you at least think about giving me another chance? I promise I won't let you down this time."

Shelby was at a loss for words. If she was pregnant with his child, out of fairness to the baby, she would have to give him another chance. Children deserved a mother and a father, preferably married. "I'll think about it. But don't pressure me."

"I promise I won't." He kissed the tips of his fingers and pressed them to her cheek. "Good luck with the wedding."

Shelby waited until he was out of sight before dropping her chin to her chest and letting the tears flow. No matter how hard she tried, she couldn't deny her feelings for him.

Grace and Wyatt were walking back to the garden house after dinner when she spotted Shelby with some guy on the dock. She stopped walking and turned to Wyatt. "I forgot. I need to ask Mom something about the wedding. Go ahead to the room without me. I won't be long."

"Don't be long. I'm ready to have my bride to myself," Wyatt said, his husky voice telling her he had sex on the brain.

Grace stood on her tiptoes to kiss him. "I can hardly wait. It's been too long. I promise, I'll hurry."

Once Wyatt had disappeared inside the garden house, Grace crept closer to the dock. From behind a palmetto tree, she got a better glimpse of the guy, who was seriously hot. She strained to listen but couldn't make out what they were saying.

The guy left in his boat, and Shelby bowed her head, swiping at her face. Was her sister crying?

Grace slipped off her sandals and walked gingerly to the end of the dock. "Shelby? Are you okay?"

"I'm fine," Shelby sniffled. "Go away, Grace."

Grace lowered herself to the edge of the dock. This has been a week for second chances. Maybe she and Shelby could start fresh as well. "I can tell you're upset, and I'd like to help."

"Why? Because your life is back to being perfect, and now you want to pick apart mine?"

Grace grimaced. Was there truth to Shelby's allegation? "I realize you and I haven't always gotten along."

Shelby huffed. "That's an understatement."

Grace sighed. This would be harder than expected. "I admit I haven't been very nice to you."

Shelby's head swiveled toward Grace. "Nice? Cinderella's evil stepsisters are nicer than you."

"Okay, I deserved that." Grace scooted closer to Shelby. "But I'm trying here. At least meet me halfway. Who's the hot guy? Was that Josh?"

Shelby remained silent for a beat as though considering whether to confide in her. "That was Matt. We had a fling when I first moved here. He rocked my world. I was really into him. And then he decided I was too young." She snapped her fingers. "And just like that, he started seeing someone else. Now he tells me he thinks he loves me. He asked me to give him another chance."

"And what about Josh?" Grace asked.

Shelby shrugged. "Josh is wonderful. Reliable and considerate and loyal."

"He's a guy, Shelby. Not a dog. Do you have feelings for him?"

"We have a different kind of chemistry. I'm definitely attracted to him. He's sweeter, gentler. He would be a good partner. Have you ever had to choose between two guys?" Shelby asked, looking over at her.

Grace held her sister's gaze, and for the first time seemingly ever, they actually saw each other. "When I met Wyatt, we were both seeing other people. My relationship with the other guy was comfortable. Like Josh, he was safe. But Wyatt and I couldn't deny our strong attraction."

"Obviously, you ended up together. Did you break the other guy's heart?" Shelby asked.

"Not for long. He started dating someone else, and now they're married. What did you tell Matt?"

"That I would think about it." Shelby shifted, tucking one leg under the other. "What do you think I should do?"

"Don't make any rash decisions. Get to know both of them better. People say to follow your heart for a reason. Because your heart knows best, and true love is nearly impossible to deny."

"But is true love all that?" Shelby asked.

Grace nodded. "Absolutely! I highly recommend it."

Shelby inhaled an unsteady breath. "Thanks for the advice."

"You're welcome." A moment of comfortable silence passed between them. "I let this wedding go to my head, and I almost lost Wyatt because of it. I've been thinking a lot about my family these past few days. I'm sorry you and I have never gotten along, but I don't think it's too late for us to start over. Would you consider being my maid of honor?"

Shelby narrowed her eyes at Grace. "Do you really want me? Or are you asking me because none of your other bridesmaids can come?"

Grace placed a hand on her sister's shoulder. "I don't want anyone else *but* you. I have a confession to make. I didn't ask you to be a bridesmaid because I was afraid you'd show me up on my wedding day. I don't think you truly understand how stunningly beautiful you are."

Shelby's brow hit her hairline. "Whoa. That's the nicest thing you've ever said to me."

"And I mean it. If you say yes to being my maid of honor, we'll go shopping at that cute little boutique in town tomorrow morning, and I'll buy you whatever dress you choose."

"Hmm. I'm skeptical about your motivations, but I would never say no to a free dress," Shelby said, and the sisters shared a rare moment of laughter.

Grace put her arm around Shelby, pulling her close. "I understand why you don't trust me. If you give me a chance, I'll prove my motivations are honorable."

As the sun dipped below the horizon, Shelby rested her head on Grace's shoulder. "I hope you mean it, Grace. There's nothing I'd like more than to be close to my big sister."

thirty-four

· · ·

Early Saturday morning, Rand texted Kate from the Charleston airport, letting her know he was coming to the wedding but asking her to keep it a secret.

When he entered the cottage, Grace's face lit up like stage lights at a Broadway show. "Daddy! You're here!"

"Of course, I'm here, sweetheart. I couldn't miss our big day."

Grace set down the makeup brush. "You didn't bring *her* with you, did you?"

"Not hardly. I value my life," he said with an awkward chuckle that neither Kate nor Grace returned.

Rand kissed Grace's cheek and stood back to admire their oldest daughter. "You look positively stunning."

Kate was not surprised when he didn't recognize her wedding gown.

"I hope you'll allow me to give you away," Rand said.

Grace cast an uncertain glance at Kate. They had decided that Kate would give Grace away in her father's absence. Grace looked relieved when Kate nodded her approval. "Yes, Daddy. I'd like that."

"I'll give you two a few minutes alone while I check on the preparations," Kate said and slipped out of the room.

Retrieving her clutch from her room, Kate smeared lipstick on her lips and checked her reflection in the mirror one last time. Grace had taken the St. Clair women on a shopping trip to Tracy's Threads yesterday morning. Shelby had chosen a gorgeous yellow silk gown that complemented her coloring and hugged her slim figure. Kate had opted for a floral chiffon dress that danced around her calves. And Izzy, insisting she cover up her old legs, had found an elegant cream-colored linen pantsuit.

Kate left the cottage and crossed the courtyard, sticking her head inside the back door. The kitchen was chaotic, with Savannah at the stove and Pritchard barking orders at the servers he'd hired. Closing the door, she proceeded to the terrace where a semicircle of white folding chairs awaited in front of a blue hydrangea-covered arbor. At the opposite end, a rectangular table was adorned with Izzy's Herend Chinese Bouquet Blue china and vases of blue hydrangeas. They were blessed with glorious weather—low humidity and temperatures in the eighties. Beyond the dunes, the sun hung high in a periwinkle sky, its rays sparkling off the calm ocean.

Kate lingered at the edge of the terrace, absorbing the scene. When she finally turned around, she noticed Silas standing in the shade of the house, watching her.

"We couldn't have asked for better weather," she said, joining him in the shade.

"You're right about that. We don't get many days like this in the Lowcountry in July. I haven't seen you since you returned. Welcome home. How're you holding up? So much has happened for you these past few weeks."

Kate chuckled. "No kidding. I'm still reeling from all the changes. I'm not starting a new chapter in my life. I'm starting a new part, the whole second half."

He chuckled. "That's a good way to look at it. I heard about your husband's affair. I'm sorry you're having to go through that."

Kate inhaled a deep breath, bringing herself to her full height.

"Don't be. My marriage has been over for some time. Rand's affair allowed me to cut ties with no guilt. Because of them, I'm free to move back here."

When a food server thrust his way out of the French doors with a Champagne bucket, Silas pulled Kate out of the way. "Hey, buddy! Watch where you're going," Silas called out to the server.

Standing so close to Silas's muscular body sent tingles down Kate's legs. A vision flashed in her mind of him kissing her in the light of a full moon. To say her summer had gotten off to a rocky start was an understatement. But she aimed to make the most of the time she had left. Maybe a sexy summer fling was just what she needed to make her feel alive again.

"Say, Silas, would you care to join us for lunch? We have plenty of food."

His smile melted her insides. "I'd like that very much. Thank you, Kate."

Trumpet Voluntary played softly from a Bluetooth speaker as Grace took her father's arm. When they stepped through the French doors onto the terrace, they were greeted by a kaleidoscope of blue—ocean, sky, hydrangeas, and table decorations. Who needed helicopter getaways and fireworks displays when she had sandy white beaches, puffy white clouds, and the sun's rays sparkling like diamonds off the deep-blue ocean waters?

As they started toward the small crowd, Grace tugged on her father's arm for him to slow down. She wanted to take it all in, to savor this moment she'd anticipated since she was a little girl. Although she had intended to invite the entire city of Austin to her wedding, she realized that all she really needed was her family gathered here.

Blossom—dressed like an angel in flowing white robes and a halo of baby's breath woven into her mop of silver coils—waited for them under the arbor. Grace hung on her every word as she spoke of the sanctity of marriage. She and Wyatt were starting their lives together as husband and wife. Once they were settled again at home, she would go off the pill and start trying to have a baby.

When Blossom pronounced them husband and wife, Wyatt planted a kiss on her that drew applause from the small crowd. Shelby placed a glass of Champagne in her hand, and the newlyweds mingled with family members until Pritchard called them to the table for lunch.

Grace and Wyatt were seated together on one side with Shelby on Grace's right and Wyatt's father on his left. Kate occupied one end, and Izzy the opposite. Her father and Wyatt's mother were seated across the table, with the rest of the family filling the other seats. While the servers presented the first course—chilled cucumber and avocado soup—Grace sipped Champagne and studied her guests. She was grateful to Pritchard and Savannah for the elegant lunch. She aimed to become better acquainted with Pritchard's family during future trips to the Lowcountry.

She leaned into Shelby. "You seem sad. Do you wish you'd asked Josh to come?"

"Not at all. I didn't want the distraction. Today is about you."

Grace tucked a stray lock of strawberry-blonde hair behind Shelby's ear. "You look amazing, by the way."

Shelby flashed a brilliant smile. "So do you. Mom's dress is perfect for you."

"I know. Can you believe it?" Grace ran her hand across the satin bodice. "Maybe you can wear it too when your time comes."

Shelby bobbed her head. "That'd be cool! We can start a tradition. Don't spill anything on it."

"I'll be careful. Now that we've put our differences aside, I hope we continue strengthening our sisterly bond. Let's stay in touch. Call me anytime. I'm here for you if ever you need advice. I have plenty of it."

Shelby laughed out loud. "Boy, do you ever." She grew serious again, tears welling in her eyes. "Thank you for asking me to be your maid of honor. It really means a lot."

Grace squeezed Shelby's arm. "You bet. I feel blessed to have three generations of St. Clair women here today."

When Shelby's gaze shifted, Grace saw her mother laughing at something Silas had said. "What's that about? Is Mom flirting with Silas?"

"Looks like it, doesn't it?" Shelby said.

A lightbulb flashed in Grace's mind. After all these weeks, she finally recognized what was so different about her mother. For the first time in years, her mother seemed genuinely happy. Her glow wasn't from the sun. It was shining from within. Was it the Lowcountry? Or ending her troubled marriage? It was probably a mixture of both.

Grace had been wrong about so many things, and she was grateful for the opportunity to start over, to make amends to those she'd hurt.

Shelby stood in the courtyard long after Grace and Wyatt left in their getaway car. They would spend two nights in Charleston before heading back to Austin. They planned to take a honeymoon in the fall to an exotic destination.

Shelby's spirits tanked when she finally headed to her room to change for work. A week ago, she'd wished her older sister lived in a faraway country. Now she resented the twelve hundred miles separating them. And she had a new brother-in-law. Wyatt had always been kind to Shelby, unlike many of Grace's previous boyfriends who treated her like a bratty kid sister.

In her room, Shelby opened her top dresser drawer and removed the pregnancy test she'd purchased at the drugstore yesterday while shopping for makeup. Her cycle was regular, and she was two days late. If she was pregnant, based on her calculations, the baby was probably Matt's. Knowing Matt, he would insist on doing the honorable thing by marrying her. But she didn't trust him. If only he were more dependable like Josh.

She dropped the pregnancy test in the drawer and slammed it shut. She would wait another day. Maybe even two or three. She wasn't ready for her life to change. She needed more time to think. She hugged herself. Secretly, she hoped she was pregnant. The notion of a baby growing inside her filled the emptiness with a comforting warmth she had never before experienced.

I hope you've enjoyed *Beneath the Carolina Sun,* the second installment in the Sandy Island series. New characters join the cast in the next in series, *Southern Simmer.* Join the Adventure Club for a deeper dive into life at Magnolia Shores—think maps, recipes, and character profiles. You'll receive a download with bonus material and much more.

If you'd like read more about Savannah and her family, be sure to check out the Marsh Point trilogy. You might also enjoy my other family drama series: Palmetto Island, Hope Springs, and Virginia Vineyards.

Use the QR code below to access my online store where you'll find bundled series and receive early access to my new releases. Buying direct means you are supporting the artist instead of big business. I appreciate you. Ashley Farley Books

Also available at Barnes and Noble, Kobo, Apple Books, Amazon, and many other online book sellers.

acknowledgments

I'm forever indebted to the many people who help bring a project to fruition. My editor, Pat Peters. My cover designer, the hardworking folks at Damonza.com. My beta readers: Alison Fauls, Anne Wolters, Laura Glenn, Jan Klein, Lisa Hudson, Lori Walton, Kathy Sinclair, Rachel Story, and Amy Connolley. Last, but certainly not least, are my select group of advanced readers who are diligent about sharing their advanced reviews prior to releases.

I'm blessed to have many supportive people in my life who offer the encouragement I need to continue my pursuit of writing. Love and thanks to my family—my mother, Joanne; my husband, Ted; and my amazing children, Cameron and Ned.

Most of all, I'm grateful to my wonderful readers for their love of women's fiction. I love hearing from you. Feel free to shoot me an email at ashleyhfarley@gmail.com or stop by my website at ashleyfarley.com for more information about my characters and upcoming releases. Don't forget to sign up for my newsletter. Your subscription will grant you exclusive content, sneak previews, and special giveaways.

about the author

Ashley Farley writes books about women for women. Her characters are mothers, daughters, sisters, and wives facing real-life issues. Her bestselling Sweeney Sisters series has touched the lives of many.

Ashley is a wife and mother of two young adult children. While she's lived in Richmond, Virginia, for the past twenty-one years, a piece of her heart remains in the salty marshes of the South Carolina Lowcountry, where she still calls home. Through the eyes of her characters, she captures the moss-draped trees, delectable cuisine, and kindhearted folk with lazy drawls that make the area so unique.

Ashley loves to hear from her readers. Visit her website @ ashleyfarley.com or online bookstore @ ashleyfarleybooks.com. Join the fun and engaged with like-minded readers in her exclusive Facebook group Georgia's Porch

Get free exclusive content by signing up for her newsletter @ ashleyfarley.com/newsletter-signup/

Made in United States
Orlando, FL
01 December 2024

54764106R00146